# MORE PRAISE FOR VERNON CRAWFORD, THE WBC PRINCIPLE, AND *FROM CONFUCIUS TO OZ*

"I strongly recommend this book for present and potential leaders in business and for people in all walks of life."
— C. B. Scrignar, M.D.
Clinical Professor of Psychiatry,
Tulane University School of Medicine

"Vernon Crawford is a creative and versatile training manager. His unique approach to management development deserves a place on every manager's bookshelf."
— Dr. Michael P. Kane,
International Training Consultant

"The WBC idea is effective in business or personal life and I have seen others apply the principles contained herein to their benefit and the benefit of others. I think everyone should read and apply this information."
— William B. Stubbs,
Corporate Training Specialist, Scrivner, Inc.

Dr. Vernon Crawford holds degrees in psychology and management, and has lectured at Tulane and Florida State. His developmental seminars have been employed by public and private organizations on a worldwide basis. Currently, he makes his home in New Orleans.

# FROM CONFUCIUS TO OZ

## THE WAY TO SUCCESS IN BUSINESS AND LIFE

### VERNON CRAWFORD

BERKLEY BOOKS, NEW YORK

This Berkley book contains the complete
text of the original hardcover edition.

FROM CONFUCIOUS TO OZ

A Berkley Book / published by arrangement with
Donald I. Fine, Inc.

PRINTING HISTORY
Donald I. Fine, Inc., edition / September 1989
Berkley trade paperback edition / March 1991

ISBN: 0-425-12616-1

PRINTED IN THE UNITED STATES OF AMERICA

10  9  8  7  6  5  4  3  2  1

## WITH SPECIAL THANKS TO:

Dr. Chet Scrignar for his ideas, encouragement, and support; Alma Crawford for her excellent typing of the manuscript; Harriett Handshaw, whose encouragement and support mean so much to me; Sammy Goh for his constructive suggestions.

# CONTENTS

# PREFACE

While preparing to teach a series of seminars in Singapore, I read the *Analects* by Confucius. In a discussion with my good friend, Dr Chet Scrignar, renowned psychiatrist, educator and author, we realized that wisdom, benevolence and courage — the virtues taught by Confucius, were in actuality the characteristics that were sought by the Scarecrow, the Tin Woodman, and the Lion, in *The Wizard of Oz*.

The universal search for wisdom, benevolence, and courage is portrayed in an extremely simple and enormously enjoyable manner in L. Frank Baum's *The Wizard of Oz*. Published in 1900, this book has become one of the most widely read children's stories in American history. The movie version, released in 1939, has become perennially popular and continues to spawn new devotees every year.

In *The Wizard of Oz*, Dorothy, blown by a tornado, suddenly found herself stranded in Oz and wanted desperately to return home to Kansas. During her odyssey, she encountered similarly wanting and memorable characters. The Scarecrow wanted brains or wisdom, because he was convinced that he could not think although he displayed ingenuity in problem-solving throughout the adventure.

# PREFACE

The Tin Woodman wanted a heart and strongly believed that he could not love. However he evinced kindness, compassion, and a concern for others all along their journey.

The Lion, during the group's trek to the Emerald City, was convinced that he lacked courage, even though he performed many brave deeds. The Lion said, 'My life is simply unbearable without a bit of courage.' He, too, thought he did not have something he already possessed.

Over 2500 years ago, Confucius pointed out that the three virtues of a successful person are Wisdom, Benevolence, and Courage. Confucius was concerned with the development of virtue and the formation of character as the basis of familial, social, and political order. He shared with modern Christianity a belief in the moral force of ideals, the Golden Rule of doing to others what you want others to do to you, honoring one's parents, and a high moral standard in human affairs. Confucius was concerned with the conduct of life in society but, was not concerned with an afterlife.

Confucianism is sometimes called a religion, however it is rather a system of ethics, or good conduct. Confucius focused his attention on making people better in this life, not in the afterlife. It is essentially an agnostic ideology, concerned with management of the visible world. With an exceptional love of learning, self-improvement and moral principles, he became the most renowned teacher in Chinese history.

No matter what your level is in an organization, what profession you practice, or what business you operate, your success depends largely on your ability to deal with other human beings. The primary duty of a manager is getting things done with and through other people. A successful manager must be able to effectively relate to other people. This is true not only for managers, but for every type of position in the modern workplace. This book is designed to help you become more effective in business and in life.

By reading and doing the exercises in this book, you will become more self-aware: aware of the way you come across to other people, and aware of how to 'read' other people. The skills you develop will help you communicate with effectiveness and power when presenting ideas, selling products, or managing people — these skills can increase productivity.

# PREFACE

In chapter 1 you will learn how to extend yourself, how to stretch your abilities, and how to become more valuable to yourself and to your organization. By doing the exercises in this chapter, you will develop powerful strategies that will give you a distinct advantage over those who have not yet learned how to manage their lives effectively. You will learn a unique planning system to reduce day-to-day crises and accomplish more in less time. You will gain greater wisdom by climbing up the wisdom ladder and using the step-by-step guide.

In chapter 2 you will learn how to respond to people with more understanding and sensitivity, how to build relationships by minimizing others' negative reactions, and how to reduce or resolve conflicts. You will gain insight into why 'drill sergeants' are losing favor and benevolent managers are winning in business today. You will increase your ability to motivate others to stretch beyond all previous performance levels, and discover the real reason why people do not give their best efforts consistently. You will develop skills in using a proven new strategy for handling people with history of negative performance or behavior.

In chapter 3 you will learn how to manage your life with confidence — without feeling guilty, anxious or uncomfortable. You will acquire the strength needed to say exactly what you mean without alienating others, realize the power of the word 'no', and learn how to use it to your advantage. You will also learn how to deal with criticism: how to give and take it. By learning and practicing these specific techniques for improving communications, you will stand up for yourself without violating the rights of others.

In the final chapter you will gain proficiency in identifying the Wisdom, Benevolence and Courage (WBC) profiles of others and become aware of how people respond to you. Applying the WBC concept will help you to realize how perception affects communication, understanding and productivity. Practicing the proven Problem Solving and Decision Making Technique will enable you to address your current on-the-job concerns and to improve your effectiveness in daily activities. By incorporating the WBC principles into your life, you will be able to create a significant impact in everything you say and do, make a positive first impression, and present yourself in such a way to obtain instant rapport.

# PREFACE

The ability and capacity for people to change their thinking, feelings and behavior has been proven by research in the behavioral sciences. History has demonstrated that people who make honest commitments can change their lives.

In order to make these changes, you must become actively involved in the process of change. Completing the questionnaire on page 14 and doing the recommended exercises are essential to the process. This is not a book to read passively. It is a powerful agent of change that requires your participation. Success becomes possible when you develop wisdom, benevolence and courage — WBC — in your character. Based on the understanding that all behavior can be changed, this book provides a plan for developing a dynamic approach to human relationships and self-improvement.

# INTRODUCTION

*He that is really wise can never be perplexed.*
*He that is really benevolent can never be unhappy.*
*He that is really courageous can never be afraid.*

Confucius

*'You have not yet told me how to get back to Kansas', said*
*Dorothy. 'Your silver shoes will carry you over the desert',*
*said the Wizard of Oz, 'you should have gone back to your*
*Aunt Em the first day you came to Oz.'*

    *'But then I should not have had my wonderful brains,'*
*cried the Scarecrow.*

    *'And I should not have had my lovely heart', said the*
*Tin Woodman.*

    *'And I should have lived a coward forever', declared*
*the Lion.*

    *Dorothy then threw her arms around the Scarecrow,*
*the Tin Woodman and the Lion, hugging and kissing them*
*all. She now took Toto up solemnly and having said one last*
*goodbye, she clapped the heels of her shoes together three*
*times saying, 'Take me home to Auntie Em.'*

The Wizard of Oz
L. Frank Baum

What is success? How can you attain it? The answer depends largely upon your concept of success. Some people say that success is wealth. They think of large mansions, chauffeur driven limousines, expensive clothes, jewelry, and all the things money can buy. Others think success is celebrity, adulation from fawning fans, instant recognition in public or being frequently mentioned in the press. For those who want to influence and control people and events, power means success. However, success is not measurable by wealth, fame, or power. These are merely some of the rewards bestowed upon successful people.

Success is reaching a goal you have set. Or, according to Webster, 'the favorable termination of a venture.' Most of us set goals; successful people reach them. Most successful people are not driven by visions of money, renown or power, although they may receive a considerable amount of each. Instead they are driven by something less tangible and more personal: the excitement of achievement. Whether it's completing a routine report or a multi-million dollar merger, achievement precedes all other rewards of success. Confucius said, 'Consider your job of prime importance; put the reward in second place — wouldn't this be excellence in its exalted form?'

Wealth, celebrity and power accrue as a consequence of success, but they are seldom mentioned by successful people as primary motivators.

Horace Greeley, American journalist and politician, placed the popularly accepted symbols of success in perspective when he said, 'Fame is vapor; popularity an accident; riches take wings. Only one thing endures and that is character.' Greeley's comment leads to a question: Is there a relationship between character and success?

Confucius addressed this question when he said: 'Possessing virtue will give the ruler the people. Possessing the people will give him territory. Possessing the territory will give him its wealth. Possessing its wealth, he will have the resources for expenditure. Virtue is the route, wealth is the result.'

Confucius aside, the attributes of wisdom, benevolence and courage have been espoused throughout the ages by philosophers, theologians, personality theorists and even writers of fairy tales. In *The Republic*, Plato (448 — 348 B.C.) wrote, 'The virtues of an ideal state are wisdom, courage and temperance. Justice is also found there. The same virtues appear in the life of a well ordered individual.'

Plato's pupil, Aristotle (384 — 322 B.C.) said, 'Wisdom is the result of training and habit; between callousness and flattery is benevolence, and between cowardice and rashness is courage.'

In Christianity, God the Father is wise, Jesus the Son who ventured forth into the world is courageous, and the Holy Ghost is the good spirit of benevolence. Sir Francis Bacon, English statesman and philosopher, wrote in *The New Atlantis* about an utopian society in which the king had a memory above all others (wisdom), a large heart wholly bent to make his kingdom happy (benevolence), and the courage to build his concept into reality.

The German philosopher Schopenhauer (1788 — 1854) wrote, 'A good will is profounder and more reliable than a clear mind.' He also said, 'All religions promise a reward for excellence of the will or heart, but none for excellence of the head or understanding.' American educator and philosopher, John Dewey, (1859 — 1952) wrote, 'Reason is "Man's imitation of divinity."' He echoed Confucius when he continued, '...and to be good does not merely mean to be obedient and harmless; goodness without ability is lame; and all of the virtue in the world will not save us if we lack intelligence.'

Carl Jung (1875 — 1961), the renowned Swiss psychiatrist, interpreted personality in terms of thought, intuition, feelings and sensing. Personality traits associated with thought and intuition are grouped under wisdom, those associated with feeling under benevolence and those with sensing under courage.

In Baum's *The Wizard of Oz*, the universal search for wisdom, benevolence and courage is portrayed at the story's end, when the unveiled but unabashed Wizard fulfills the wishes of his beseechers by validating the Scarecrow's wisdom, the Tin Woodman's benevolence, and the Lion's courage.

## WBC and Success

We all know that in real life, no wizard confirms wisdom, benevolence or courage. The capacity for wisdom lies within all of us and can be developed if we are willing to repeatedly climb the wisdom ladder. The rungs of the ladder are goal setting, learning, study, implementation, experience and judgement.

Goalsetting, a well-known strategy for achievement, must be accompanied by learning, study and implementation. Sound judgement evolves out of experience, and like wisdom, is an acquired characteristic. Successful people do not necessarily have extremely high intelligence levels, but they are committed to diligently climbing the wisdom ladder.

Benevolence is the most overlooked and ignored characteristic of success. Perhaps cliches such as 'nice guys finish last' tend to undermine the time-tested truth of the Golden Rule. Benevolence isn't weakness or letting others trample you. As Confucius said: 'Do not impose on others what you yourself do not desire. Discover what other people do or do not want done to them.' A sense of right and wrong and a concern for others, qualities mentioned in Gallup's survey of successful people, epitomize benevolence. Benevolence pays off because it makes you and the people around you feel good. It fosters self-respect and a feeling of self-worth, the absence of which makes the other fruits of success hollow and meaningless.

Wisdom and benevolence may make you self-satisfied, but without courage, you cannot be successful. The faint-hearted seldom succeed. Courage means assertiveness and the willingness to take risks. It also means self-reliance and inventiveness. But unconventional thinking and innovation invite criticism, and courage is required — courage to withstand adverse comments and the possibility of failure. Independent thought, self-confidence, and other courageous characteristics separate the successful from the unsuccessful. The application of courage is absolutely necessary if you are to reach your goals. Courage is an indispensable component in the character and behavior of successful people. However, unbridled courage becomes recklessness.

Alone, neither great wisdom, sincere benevolence nor unlimited courage will assure success. Only the incorporation of all three into your attitudes and actions will help you reach your goals and attain success.

The secret of success, as described by learned thinkers like Confucius, and personified by the quest of the Scarecrow, the Tin

# INTRODUCTION

Woodman and the Lion in *The Wizard of Oz*, lies within your character. If you mix wisdom, benevolence and courage into your thinking, your attitudes will change. In turn, your behavior will be modified and thusly, your opportunities for success will expand.

WBC people have more fun because they perceive life as an adventure, sometimes serene, sometimes unpredictable, sometimes difficult, but always a challenge. Successful people in all walks of life have developed, blended and applied WBC as they marched toward their goals.

After reading this book, you may or may not become a millionaire, a well-known celebrity, or a wielder of great power; but one thing is certain; the development of WBC in your character will make you a happier and more successful person.

# WBC QUESTIONNAIRE

*Wisdom, benevolence and courage: these are the three universal virtues. Some practice them with the ease of nature; some for the sake of their own advantage; and some by dint of great effort.*

Confucius

*I don't know anything. You see I am stuffed, so I have no brains at all.*

The Scarecrow

*When I was in love, I was the happiest man on earth; but no one can love who has not a heart.*

The Tin Woodman

*My life is simply unbearable without a bit of courage.*

The Cowardly Lion

*'Have you any brains?' asked the Scarecrow of the Lion. 'I suppose so. I've never looked to see,' replied the Lion. 'The King of Beasts shouldn't be a coward,' said the Scarecrow. 'I know it,' said the Lion, wiping a tear from his eye with the tip of his tail, 'but whenever there is danger, my heart begins to beat fast.' 'You ought to be glad,' said the Tin Woodman, for it proves you have a heart.' 'Perhaps,' said the Lion thoughtfully, 'if I had no heart I should not be a coward.'*

The Wizard of Oz
L. Frank Baum

Wisdom, benevolence and courage are essential elements of character. They are traits which we learn and their influence on our character changes with time and circumstance. In resolving to increase your wisdom, benevolence and courage, you must discover your current WBC strengths and weaknesses.

How? Constructive comments from friends, colleagues and even strangers might help. Comments such as, 'You should study more and you will be better prepared.' Or, 'If you act more kindly towards others, you will achieve your objectives more readily.' Or, 'Be more courageous, take more risks and things will work out alright.' But such statements are seldom uttered; and even if they are, you'll probably still doubt your own WBC, because it's almost impossible for others to accurately assess your virtues and vices without bias. Separating fatuous praise from genuine compliments is difficult and criticism, constructive or otherwise, is seldom made in our presence.

Unlike friends and acquaintances, the WBC Questionnaire which follows is objective and unbiased. It measures your attitudes about: 1) ideas (requiring wisdom); 2) people (requiring benevolence); 3) accomplishments (requiring courage). The questionnaire will determine your strengths and weaknesses in these three areas and give you important insights into your character.

The results of this self-analysis may surprise you, pleasantly or not. But your WBC-Q scores will stimulate your thoughts, cause you to look within yourself, and lead to a commitment for self improvement. Above all, do not dwell on a low score or ruminate about your weaknesses. Instead, prepare yourself for positive change. With your WBC-Q scores in hand, you can begin to act.

After you complete the WBC questionaire, tabulate your scores to discover your WBC profile. Compare it to other WBC profiles and become familiar with all of them. Being able to determine other WBC profiles can guide your thinking, change your attitudes, and alter your behavior as you develop effective strategies to reach your goals. Subsequent chapters in this book deal specifically with ways to acquire more wisdom, develop more benevolence, and act more courageously.

## INSTRUCTIONS

The WBC Questionnaire contains 21 self-descriptive statements. On the scale below each statement, you are to circle a number from 1 (least like you) to 10 (most like you). Answer each question honestly and quickly. Do not over-analyze. Your first response is usually your most accurate response.

## WBC QUESTIONNAIRE

1. I like to create a first impression as being friendly and understanding.

| 1 | 2 | 3 | 4 | 5 | 6 | 7 | 8 | 9 | 10 |
|---|---|---|---|---|---|---|---|---|----|

Least
like
you

Most
like
you

2. I prefer using data, analysis, reason and logic to make decisions.

| 1 | 2 | 3 | 4 | 5 | 6 | 7 | 8 | 9 | 10 |
|---|---|---|---|---|---|---|---|---|----|

Least
like
you

Most
like
you

3. When conversing with a business associate, I become impatient with talk that does not get to the point.

| 1 | 2 | 3 | 4 | 5 | 6 | 7 | 8 | 9 | 10 |
|---|---|---|---|---|---|---|---|---|----|

Least
like
you

Most
like
you

4. At times I impress others as acting too impulsively.

| 1 | 2 | 3 | 4 | 5 | 6 | 7 | 8 | 9 | 10 |
|---|---|---|---|---|---|---|---|---|---|

Least
like
you

Most
like
you

5. In written communications to an individual I do not know, I usually include all data needed to thoroughly support my position.

| 1 | 2 | 3 | 4 | 5 | 6 | 7 | 8 | 9 | 10 |
|---|---|---|---|---|---|---|---|---|---|

Least
like
you

Most
like
you

6. I listen with empathy and compassion.

| 1 | 2 | 3 | 4 | 5 | 6 | 7 | 8 | 9 | 10 |
|---|---|---|---|---|---|---|---|---|---|

Least
like
you

Most
like
you

7. I make decisions based on how people are affected.

| 1 | 2 | 3 | 4 | 5 | 6 | 7 | 8 | 9 | 10 |
|---|---|---|---|---|---|---|---|---|---|

Least
like
you

Most
like
you

8. I like others to see me as a dependable individual who gets things done.

| 1 | 2 | 3 | 4 | 5 | 6 | 7 | 8 | 9 | 10 |
|---|---|---|---|---|---|---|---|---|---|

Least
like
you

Most
like
you

9. I prefer carrying out carefully organized, detailed plans with precision.

| 1 | 2 | 3 | 4 | 5 | 6 | 7 | 8 | 9 | 10 |
|---|---|---|---|---|---|---|---|---|---|
| Least like you | | | | | | | | | Most like you |

10. When a peer does a favor for me, my immediate response is a feeling of appreciation and gratitude.

| 1 | 2 | 3 | 4 | 5 | 6 | 7 | 8 | 9 | 10 |
|---|---|---|---|---|---|---|---|---|---|
| Least like you | | | | | | | | | Most like you |

11. When confronted with a problem, I like to develop several alternative solutions and then carefully weigh the pros and cons of each.

| 1 | 2 | 3 | 4 | 5 | 6 | 7 | 8 | 9 | 10 |
|---|---|---|---|---|---|---|---|---|---|
| Least like you | | | | | | | | | Most like you |

12. I find it easier to convince others when I am concise and to the point.

| 1 | 2 | 3 | 4 | 5 | 6 | 7 | 8 | 9 | 10 |
|---|---|---|---|---|---|---|---|---|---|
| Least like you | | | | | | | | | Most like you |

13. I form opinions about people based on my gut-level feelings.

| 1 | 2 | 3 | 4 | 5 | 6 | 7 | 8 | 9 | 10 |
|---|---|---|---|---|---|---|---|---|----|

Least like you — Most like you

14. I charge into new projects, full speed ahead

| 1 | 2 | 3 | 4 | 5 | 6 | 7 | 8 | 9 | 10 |
|---|---|---|---|---|---|---|---|---|----|

Least like you — Most like you

15. When conditions prevent me from doing what I want, I analyse any deficiencies in my plan and modify them accordingly.

| 1 | 2 | 3 | 4 | 5 | 6 | 7 | 8 | 9 | 10 |
|---|---|---|---|---|---|---|---|---|----|

Least like you — Most like you

16. I usually consider every possible angle for a long time before and after making a decision.

| 1 | 2 | 3 | 4 | 5 | 6 | 7 | 8 | 9 | 10 |
|---|---|---|---|---|---|---|---|---|----|

Least like you — Most like you

17. I freely communicate my thoughts and emotions to others.

| 1 | 2 | 3 | 4 | 5 | 6 | 7 | 8 | 9 | 10 |
|---|---|---|---|---|---|---|---|---|----|

Least like you — Most like you

18. I impress others as being assertive and a quick decision maker.

| 1 | 2 | 3 | 4 | 5 | 6 | 7 | 8 | 9 | 10 |
|---|---|---|---|---|---|---|---|---|----|

Least
like
you

Most
like
you

19. People see me as logical.

| 1 | 2 | 3 | 4 | 5 | 6 | 7 | 8 | 9 | 10 |
|---|---|---|---|---|---|---|---|---|----|

Least
like
you

Most
like
you

20. People consider me to be a kind person.

| 1 | 2 | 3 | 4 | 5 | 6 | 7 | 8 | 9 | 10 |
|---|---|---|---|---|---|---|---|---|----|

Least
like
you

Most
like
you

21. People say I am an action-oriented person.

| 1 | 2 | 3 | 4 | 5 | 6 | 7 | 8 | 9 | 10 |
|---|---|---|---|---|---|---|---|---|----|

Least
like
you

Most
like
you

## WBC QUESTIONNAIRE SCORING SHEET

Instructions: Transfer your scores for each item to the appropriate blanks. Then total the scores for each dimension.

| WISDOM | BENEVOLENCE | COURAGE |
|---|---|---|
| 2_____ | 1_____ | 3_____ |
| 5_____ | 6_____ | 4_____ |
| 9_____ | 7_____ | 8_____ |
| 11_____ | 10_____ | 12_____ |
| 15_____ | 13_____ | 14_____ |
| 16_____ | 17_____ | 18_____ |
| 19_____ | 20_____ | 21_____ |
| _____ Total | _____ Total | _____ Total |

Score Interpretation:

56 — 70   Your dominant dimension

42 — 55   Some strength in this dimension

10 — 41   Weakness in this dimension

# WBC QUESTIONNAIRE

Consider only scores between 56—70. Your highest score is your most dominant dimension; the next highest score between 56—70 is your secondary dimension. Do not consider any scores below 56 as dominant or secondary dimensions.

In the event of tie scores above 56, dimensions are interpreted equally. If no scores are above 56, continue to add 7 to each of your three scores until at least one score is above 56.
For example:

If you scored 60 on Wisdom, 56 on Courage and 40 on Benevolence, then your dominant dimension is Wisdom and your secondary dimension is Courage. Benevolence is your least dominant dimension.

## IDENTIFY YOUR PROFILE:

**Wisdom (W)** — Wisdom above 56. Benevolence and Courage below 56.

**Wisdom-Benevolence (WB)** — Wisdom above Benevolence, both scores above 56. Courage below 56.

**Wisdom-Courage (WC)** — Wisdom above Courage, both scores above 56. Benevolence below 56.

**Benevolence (B)** — Benevolence above 56. Wisdom and Courage below 56.

**Benevolence-Wisdom (BW)** — Benevolence above Wisdom, both scores above 56. Courage below 56.

**Benevolence-Courage (BC)** — Benevolence above Courage, both scores above 56. Wisdom below 56.

**Courage (C)** — Courage above 56. Wisdom and Benevolence below 56.

**Courage-Wisdom (CW)** — Courage above Wisdom, both scores above 56. Benevolence below 56.

**Courage-Benevolence (CB)** — Courage above Benevolence, both scores above 56. Wisdom below 56.

**Wisdom-Benevolence-Courage (WBC)** — All scores above 56.

However, if there is a 7-point spread or better between your top score and your bottom score, then your bottom score is not considered a secondary dimension.

## INTERPRETATION

After identifying your WBC profile, read the appropriate interpretation. Remember, your profile is not immutable, but rather serves to identify your strengths and weaknesses. Wisdom, benevolence and courage are not static qualities. They are dynamic and depend upon your circumstances and desires. As you read your profile, analyze your non-dominant characteristics. To set a course for self-improvement, complete the developmental exercises found in the succeeding chapters.

After you read your own WBC profile, become familiar with the rest of the profiles. People you know will come to mind when you read the other combinations of WBC. You can interact with others more effectively when you are aware of their WBC profiles.

## WISDOM

Within the context of this book, wisdom means a systematized collection of data. Methodical learning and studying, and thorough analysis of information are characteristics of wise people. Logic and reason prevail when they solve problems. But wisdom is not synonymous with intelligence, although intelligent people may possess many W characteristics. W s are logical and precise, like computers, but they often lack the human virtues of benevolence and courage.

### Wisdom (W)

Ws are logical, analytical and introverted. Objective in their observations of people and events, Ws rarely succumb to emotional appeals. They are deliberate in their decision-making, carefully weighing the pros and cons of each alternative. Ws are often meticulous, preferring details and precision. They draw conclusions based on fact.

Extreme Ws are insensitive to others and are reticent about expressing their own emotions. Considered shy by some, these Ws prefer to withdraw into their own thoughts. In order to make a decision, the extreme W collects reams of data, over-analyzes the situation, and then, in a quandary of indecisiveness, fails to act. The world of concepts and ideas supercedes involvement with people and accomplishing tasks.

## Wisdom-Benevolence (WB)

The WB is astute in identifying and analyzing the existing feelings, values, beliefs and motives of others. The WB's need is to withdraw into themselves to collect and analyze data; yet this is tempered by the desire to socialize. These antithetical forces balance each other to create what Aristotle called the 'Golden Mean', or the medium between extremes. WBs are well organized and fastidious, and they keep work areas tidy and personal appearance neat.

An extreme WB is reluctant to take risks and will do so only after collecting all the facts and gaining the support of friends, family, peers and supervisors. Decisions are distasteful for the WB. He prefers collecting data and having a committee make decisions. Analysis and a concern for others take precedence over accomplishment.

## Wisdom-Courage (WC)

When confronted with a problem, WCs collect data, develop several solutions, and after carefully weighing the pros and cons of each, implement the best solution. They plan pragmatically and systematically, developing strategies and tactics for tangible results. The WC shows a good memory for facts and figures, careful attention to details, and the ability to make objective evaluations.

An overly zealous WC is overpowering, lacking in trust and unmerciful. The feelings and values of others often are not noticed or understood. The WC tends to be too forceful when persuading others and tries to bend people to his will. Because the extreme WC is serious, rigid, stubborn and opinionated, he sometimes must be forced to change direction. The WC prefers to work long hours, and is not interested in social events, family gatherings or pleasing others.

## BENEVOLENCE

Benevolence, an often elusive but highly desired quality, signifies a warm heart. Compassion, kindness and a regard for others characterize benevolent people. Without benevolence, the ability to lead others is seriously hampered. The growth and development of an organization is severely limited, and the fostering of happiness and contentment is impaired. In the successful person, benevolence must be properly mixed with wisdom and courage. Otherwise, sentimentality may supercede reason and logic, leaving emotion to govern decisions. Often, the presence or absence of benevolence determines success or failure of an endeavor.

## Benevolence (B)

Kindness, generosity and concern for others characterize the B person. Bs prefer longstanding, intimate relationships; Bs are tenaciously loyal to their spouses, friends, and employers. They listen with empathy and understanding and draw out the feelings of others. Bs make decisions on an emotional level instead of relying on facts and logic. They are sensitive to the effect of their actions on others.

A person with B characteristics and low W and C dimensions strikes others as subjective, sentimental and weak. B people can easily be manipulated by hard luck stories, teary eyes, wagging tails and other emotional appeals. The typical B avoids confrontation, is indirect when making proposals or giving assignments, and is ambivalent about disciplining others. Frequently, Bs are overly tolerant of poor service and non-producers.

## Benevolence-Courage (BC)

BCs work well with others to accomplish goals. They genuinely like people and achieve their objectives through teamwork. On committees, they act as catalysts and as cohesive forces, while motivating other members. Extroverted and direct, BC types work well when challenged by an assignment which requires the cooperation of others.

BCs with a weak W may be Pollyannas, over-zealous about the potential of subordinates. They charge forward, ignoring logic and reason, making decisions based on emotion and other's perceptions of their actions. When given a routine task that does not involve others, the BC quickly becomes impulsive, impatient and lonely — often ceasing work to seek companionship.

## Benevolence-Wisdom (BW)

BWs astutely identify the motives of others. They have keen insight into their own needs, values, opinions, beliefs and desires. On first meetings, they are friendly and congenial while silently evaluating the potential of a genuine relationship. Traditional values and natural conservatism make a BW a loyal friend, spouse or employee. Because BWs are empathetic, compassionate and understanding, and develop logical solutions to personal problems, many people seek their counsel.

When you meet a BW with an extremely low C score, you might feel attracted yet curiously distanced. BWs focus on relationships and the collection of information; accomplishing goals is secondary. A committee composed entirely of BWs will have a grand old time and develop a lot of plans, but will be slow to actually accomplish objectives.

## COURAGE

Without wisdom, the plan is not seen to fruition; without benevolence, there is no concern for fellow humans; but without courage, nothing gets done. Courage is essential in reaching a goal. Taking risks requires courage in facing the possibility of failure. No one hopes to become inured to criticism and the prospect of failure, but courageous people nevertheless persist in their objectives. Courage not tempered with wisdom and benevolence, however, is reckless, rude and to be avoided.

### Courage (C)

People with this profile are action-oriented in both making decisions and accomplishing goals. Very much the 'here and now' type, Cs are not anxious about past decisions or concerned about future development. Cs exude self-confidence and are fiercely independent. They need little external motivation for accomplishment; they are self-starters and strive for concrete results.

Extreme C types may be impulsive, shortsighted and narrow. They are impulsive when they make decisions without collecting sufficient data or thoroughly analyzing the situation; shortsighted when they fail to consider the long-range impact of present actions; and narrow when they do not take into consideration the human consequences of their actions. Forcefulness, bluntness and callousness characterize a C's personal relationships.

## Courage-Wisdom (CW)

CWs tenaciously pursue an independent path toward fixed goals. Dogged determination, attention to detail and follow-through are C traits, but the CW's chief desire is to get the job done in a logical, ordered way. They do well with challenging technical assignments and respond to action and logic rather than emotion.

Pleasing others is one of a CW's last priorities; he may be direct, blunt, tactless and callous. CWs are dispassionate about people, yet passionate about doing a job on schedule and as planned. Conflicting emotions abound within the CW; when given a task, his urgent need to complete it competes with his need for more information before getting started.

## Courage-Benevolence (CB)

CBs intensely desire accomplishment, yet possess a genuine interest and concern for the welfare of others. They strive to get the job done in a friendly way. On committees, CBs motivate others to accomplish tasks with zeal and humour. CBs are adept at getting others to help with repetitious and time-consuming projects.

CBs who score extremely low in W do not plan as thoroughly as they should and tend to make subjective decisions without adequate information. In the CB psyche, the sense of urgency collides with a fear of hurting someone's feelings. Complicated, time-consuming tasks that require individual effort frustrate the CB; when faced with such a task, he becomes inept and disorganized.

## WISDOM-BENEVOLENCE-COURAGE (WBC)

A WBC profile indicates a well-adjusted but not perfect individual. A WBC brings to mind the motto of Alcoholics Anonymous: 'God grant me the serenity to accept the things I cannot change, the courage to change the things I can, and the wisdom to know the difference.' WBCs know that work and study are necessary for accomplishment. When things go wrong, they look to themselves for remedies. WBCs are aware of human frailties and know that nurture comes through kindly direction, warmth and caring. Individuals with a WBC profile possess drive and perseverance, and are assertive in relationships. They are self-confident and gutsy; they take calculated chances and assume risks. WBCs use judgement, common sense and a blend of wisdom, benevolence and courage to solve problems. Flexibility, not dogmatic rigidity, combines with astuteness, good-heartedness and persistence in the character of a WBC.

WBCs plan work in a logical, objective manner. They are interested in others' feelings and can motivate others, but the need to please is tempered with the drive to accomplish goals. They plan well and accomplish goals by influencing others in a positive way.

A balanced profile is unique. The WBCs are not super-humans or miracle workers, but they do possess insight into their own character and the personalities of others. Most of all, balanced WBCs have an abiding faith in themselves, a concern for others, and a strong desire to get things done.

# CLIMBING THE WISDOM LADDER

*To love virtue and not learning: a simpleton*
*To love knowing and not learning: shallowness*
*To love honesty and not learning: naivete*
*To love plain speech and not learning: rudeness*
*To love physical strength and not learning: rebelliousness*
*To love determination and not learning: recklessness*

Confucius

*'Can you give me some brains?' asked the Scarecrow.*
*'You don't need them,' said the Wizard. 'You are*
*learning something every day. A baby has brains, but it*
*doesn't know much.'*
*'Experience is the only thing that brings knowledge.*
*The longer you are on earth, the more experience you are*
*sure to get.'*

The Wizard of Oz
L. Frank Baum

We are not born wise. Confucius, having said 'Those who are born with knowledge are the highest,' admitted that he had never met such a person. Few of us consciously set as a goal 'to become wise'. Instead, we aspire to build a better mouse-trap, to develop a useful service or product, or to achieve a well-defined goal. We accumulate wisdom during the process of attaining a goal. Businessmen, physicians, lawyers, artisans, philosophers, writers and mechanics acquire wisdom as they learn and study their crafts.

There are six steps to attaining wisdom.

1. Goal setting
2. Learning or acquiring knowledge from others.
3. Studying or using data acquired from others or by yourself to solve a problem.
4. Implementation or the application of learning and studying.
5. Experience derived from implementation.
6. Judgement derived from all of the preceding steps.

Obviously, the acquisition of wisdom requires a lot of effort, but it is not drudgery. Successful people enjoy work and consider acquiring wisdom a benefit of the job.

## THE WISDOM LADDER

Everyone who is successful climbs the wisdom ladder. Sometimes, the climb is straight and quick; sometimes it is slow and circuitous. But it is always an adventure. Confucius said, 'Is it not pleasant to learn with unfailing perserverance and application?' No matter what your job, learning to climb the wisdom ladder will make you more successful.

### Step 1 — Goal Setting

The first rung on the wisdom ladder is goal setting. if we don't know where we want to go, we become apathetic—any place will do. Going through life with no goals in mind is like going through life without vision. Goals create a vision of our future achievements.

Opportunities can be grasped only when they are perceived and they are perceived within a context of knowing what is wanted. Goals must be clearly defined. The more ambiguous the picture, the more unlikely it is that one will be able to respond positively to opportunities that arise.

Have you ever been exposed to 'lazy thinking' either as a speaker or listener? Lazy thinking refers to thoughts that are non-specific, disorganized, illogical and usually precede pointless speech. The words sound all right, but they convey no meaning in terms of instruction or information. Lazy thinking is not a manifestation of mental illness. It is careless and unsystematic thinking and leads to words and speech almost incomprehensible to others. An unclear mind and fuzzy thinking leads to unclear goals and fuzzy objectives.

Have you ever given someone instructions when your objectives were not clear in your own mind? All of us have. The results are usually unsatisfactory, or even disastrous. Frequently bosses berate puzzled subordinates for a failure to carry out instructions when the orders themselves were unclear or ambiguous. It is amazing how many people are unaware of the equation: lazy thinking + lazy talk = failure.

Clear and concise thinking requires an analytic mind honed by learning and study. When plans are well thought out and specific goals defined, the probability of attainment rises. As simple as it is, many people ignore this first important step of setting a specific goal and formulating logical steps to achieve the goal.

By setting specific goals, we focus on what we need to learn. No one can develop wisdom about everything there is to know in the world.

## Step 2 — Learning

Once your goals are defined, the next step is the acquisition of data. Research, learning what is already known about a subject, forms the foundation for wisdom. Investigation involves an analysis of previous attempts to develop, manufacture, or merchandise the product or service under consideration. You don't need to be a genius or have a degree from an Ivy League college in order to learn. In fact, too much theory may impede success in business, considering the importance of pragmatism. A desire to learn and a commitment to the learning process are important prerequisites to wisdom.

Anyone can learn from any life experience; however, books, journals, magazines, articles and reports are the traditional sources of data. Recent advances in computers and satellite transmission speed data throughout the world. Satellite communications offer us access to any given field. Video and audio educational cassettes present facts once available only in written media. Formal education offers another opportunity for the acquisition of data and the interchange of ideas. We also obtain information from colleagues and peers during casual conversations or at business meetings.

Learning is indeed a lifelong process. Learning means involvement in life and that is rewarding in itself. The pathway to success must be paved with knowledge. Confucius said, 'To be fond of learning is near to wisdom,' and 'the wise man is never of two minds.' Knowledge is power; ambiguities abate and decisions are made easier when you have the appropriate information.

## Step 3 — Study

Learning is the acquisition of data. Studying is using data to make decisions. For example, you learn how to add, subtract, multiply and divide. However, you must study to use mathematics in solving an engineering problem. The evaluation of data and the consideration of alternatives in solving problems is the essence of study.

Study, purposeful thinking, is essential in the acquisition of wisdom. Without study, goals will not be achieved. Confucius said, 'If one learns but does not think, one will be bewildered. If one thinks but does not learn from others, one will be imperiled.'

Study molds ideas into a plan for action. When some of us think of studying we remember only homework and study halls. As we grow older however, we find study can be more rewarding than play. Anyone who has come up with a new idea or a better way to do something can attest to the wonderful feeling of creativity. Successful people thrive on accomplishments which make work seem like play. The presence or absence of study can determine success or failure.

## Step 4 — Implementation

Unused knowledge represents a waste of the most precious human commodity — creativity. An idea not acted upon is like a crop not harvested. The challenge of implementing ideas can induce apprehension, anxiety and self-doubt, which can inhibit action. No one benefits from the failure to act. What separates people who apply their knowledge from dreamers who fantasize and procrastinate? The answer is COURAGE (See chapter 3).

People who fear failure, disapproval or rejection may not attain their goals. Those who pave the way for progress travel an uncharted, uncertain course. Fortunately, the exhilaration of achievement through implementation of what has been learned and studied quickly reverses feelings of anxiety.

## Step 5 — Experience

What is experience? According to Webster's Dictionary, it is 'the state or result of being engaged in an activity or in affairs, and results from knowledge, skill, or practice derived from direct observation or participation in events.' Experience evolves from learning, studying and implementing. Doctors get experience by treating patients, lawyers by trying cases, and businessmen by conducting transactions. One often hears: 'There's no substitute for experience.'

Although it takes time to get experience, it is not the private property of the aged. Diligence and careful attention, more than age, bring experience. Anyone who applies knowledge consistently acquires experience.

## Step 6 — Judgement

Alfred North Whitehead, mathematician and philosopher, once said, 'Intelligence is the... capacity to act wisely on the thing apprehended.' Acting wisely requires judgement, often referred to as common sense. Common sense is the ability to make sound decisions, and is developed by making numerous trips up the wisdom ladder. Good judgement results from learning, studying, applying knowledge and gaining experience through repetition. Confucius said, 'All men are alike in their nature, but become more different through practice.'

Good judgement cannot be learned from books alone nor can it be passed from one person to another. Good judgement is acquired through experience. It is developed by: 1) carefully defining a problem; 2) exploring alternatives; 3) weighing the consequences; 4) choosing the best alternative; and 5) analyzing the results of your choice in order to make a better decision in the future. The more you practice the process, the better your judgement becomes. These steps are analyzed in more detail later in this chapter.

In many respects, wisdom is synonymous with good judgement. We seek the advice of people with good judgement. They are perceived as being innately wise; however, this obfuscates the basic facts that hard work and experience make us healthy, wealthy and wise.

## WISDOM AND SUCCESS

Successful people climb the wisdom ladder repeatedly as they establish different priorities and set new goals. Wisdom cannot be acquired hastily. Confucius said, 'Do not be desirous to have things done quickly; do not look at small advantages. Desire to have things done quickly prevents them from being done thoroughly. Looking at small advantages prevents great efforts from being accomplished.' Patience, planning and practice are essential components of wisdom. 'When the mind was disciplined and expanded by study,' Confucius said, 'the remarkable harmonies of nature would become plain. One has to fill oneself with knowledge like a vessel. Upon the knowledge gained, the indwelling truth would act like a yeast, forcing the mind to assume its original perfect shape.' When your mind is disciplined and you have climbed the six steps of the wisdom ladder, you can become wiser. You may ask, 'If this is true, why are there not more wise people in the world?' The truth is there are many wise people in the world and you can become one of them if you will apply the principles found in this chapter.

## A CASE HISTORY

Nothing condemns a manager more than being labeled disorganized. A disorganized manager has no clear goals, jumps from one activity to another without apparent reason, arrives late for meetings and appointments, loses paperwork, and misses deadlines.

Different levels of management require different abilities to plan and organize. The first-level supervisor must have good technical and interpersonal skills, while upper level supervisors must have effective planning skills. Supervisors who rise in management without developing an ability to plan and organize work may fall prey to the Peter Principle: rising until they reach their level of incompetence.

If you feel you are a victim of the Peter Principle, you can change. The following case study illustrates how one supervisor's advancement into areas in which he had little wisdom affected his job performance, family life and personal well-being. It also shows that, having been promoted to his level of incompetence, this man could improve his performance by applying wisdom.

## Nick

After receiving his industrial technology degree, Nick went to work in the drafting department of a large manufacturing facility. A hard worker, loyal to his friends, family, and employer, Nick liked his work and always went the extra mile to do a job properly and on time. This won him the respect of both his boss and his peers. After five years as a draftsman, Nick was given responsibility for supervising eight employees. During the next six years, Nick's drafting unit broke all established production records. Then, Nick was promoted to section manager, a job that required planning, directing, organizing and controlling 32 employees. During the next four quarters, Nick's drafting unit missed production quotas. Materials did not arrive on time, he was short of manpower, and costs frequently ran over budget. Nick always seemed to have a crisis at hand; he was continually putting out fires. After a series of reprimands, Nick's manager referred him for counseling.

During counseling, Nick blamed most of his problems on paperwork. As a section manager, he had to requisition materials and equipment, expedite them, forecast needs and make the budget. This took a lot of time and with each fiscal quarter, Nick fell further behind in his work. He said paperwork made him miss deadlines. Although Nick worked 50 hours each week, deadlines caused him to make impulsive decisions. The stress at work made it hard for Nick to relax even at home. He began to fear for his section and his job. When the company decided to increase productivity, Nick became very anxious. He was afraid his employees would turn against him if he insisted they work more quickly.

Forecasting the budget was a complicated, time-consuming task which frustrated and disorganized Nick. His personal finances were also a mess — his checkbook wouldn't balance, and he was overdrawn at the bank. One of his five children had reached college age, but Nick had not made any plans for her education. Nick frequently complained of headaches, lower back pain and a nervous stomach.

Nick also felt that he was not keeping abreast of current developments in technology. Many of his company's competitors had automated their drafting departments, making them more productive than Nick's section. But Nick had no time to study automation and his knowledge of drafting had become outdated.

## Nick's WBC

On the WBC-Q Nick scored 64 on courage, 59 on benevolence and 35 on wisdom. His CB profile fitted him: a man who worked hard to do his job in a friendly manner. His inability to organize, plan and analyze were characteristic of a low W. Nick liked action and instead of working on significant issues, he jumped aimlessly from one small task to another.

In *The Nature of Management Work*, H. Mintzberg studied a number of managers at work and found that most of their days were filled with action and interruptions. Managerial activity was usually brief, ranging from 48 seconds to two minutes per activity. For one group of managers, Mintzberg found that only 12 times in 35 days did they work undisturbed for at least 23 minutes. But this group was able to identify goals, set priorities and manage time. After several counseling sessions, Nick recognized his own need to develop those abilities.

As a supervisor, Nick required different skills than those he needed as a section manager. As a supervisor, Nick's drive and his ability to motivate subordinates had served him well. But when he became section manager, he required more wisdom. Planning became a major activity and this was something Nick had never done, at work or at home. As a section manager, he had to meet with clients to determine their needs, work with engineering to determine specifications, and forecast manpower and material requirements. It became necessary, therefore, for Nick to plan and set priorities to achieve his objectives.

The world of drafting, like other professions, has been revolutionized by the computer. Some of Nick's anxiety had been created by his fear of automation. Nick would need a working knowledge of software and technological terminology in order to use computers. Nick felt he wasn't smart enough to meet this new demand of his job.

A plan was developed for Nick to expand his wisdom. The first exercise consisted of setting goals — for the next month, for one year, and for his lifetime. Nick's lifetime goals were: to manage a highly productive drafting section, and to finance his children's education. His one-year goals were to complete at least one course in drafting automation, and to save at least 10 percent of his annual income for his children's education. His immediate goals were to find a school that offered automation courses and to begin investing for his children's education.

With goals set, Nick began to keep a time inventory of his activities for the next week. At week's end, Nick found he had wasted time with drop-in visitors, telephone conversations and meetings. He saw that he procrastinated over tasks involving individual effort and detailed work. Nick often deliberately avoided unpleasant tasks by inviting interruptions. When the deadline for a budget or forecast drew near, Nick found increasing amounts of time for visitors, meetings and phone calls. At home, television was consuming three hours of Nick's time every night.

After keeping a time inventory for one week, Nick decided to:

1. Limit phone conversations to five minutes when possible.
2. Organize his files for quick access to documents.
3. Begin the most dreaded tasks first and engage in more enjoyable work later.
4. Limit television viewing and use that time to attend school to study automation.

## Results

Changes in Nick's work habits, his lifestyle and his ability to make sound judgements did not occur overnight. Daily, he worked diligently and deliberately to effect permanent change. He got down to business within the first minute of a telephone conversation, and avoided personal comments. (After a few weeks of practice, this new telephone etiquette became natural!) He asked his secretary to organize his files, and began to learn her system. Setting priorities, keeping a daily 'to do' list, and doing the most dreaded tasks first helped Nick to stop procrastinating. Study replaced television as his evening activity.

In the following months, Nick became more effective and efficient in his job. The telephone became a time saver, rather than a time waster. Organized files made it easy to find information. When his boss or a client asked for historical data, Nick retrieved the data readily. Missed deadlines became a thing of the past. With his current knowledge of automation, Nick was able to convince the company to automate his drafting section. The drawings that had once taken weeks were now produced in days. Change orders for products could now be made in seconds.

After an outstanding three years, Nick was promoted and given a sizeable pay increase. With his additional income, he was able to contribute more money to his children's education. As he gained more control of his environment, he became much more relaxed.

**If Nick Can, You Can Too!**
For the last 10 years, I have used goal setting and time inventory in counseling sessions and seminars all over the world. The results are the same, whether conducted in Western Europe, Southeast Asia, or the United States. My students say these simple exercises are the very valuable lessons. They report a new clarity in their thinking and are astonished that they wasted time doing things that had little relationship to their real goals. The goal setting exercise which follows will focus your attention on specific, primary goals and will help you discover what you really want from life. The time inventory will help you effectively use time to achieve your goals.

**GOAL SETTING**
In *The Wizard of Oz*, Dorothy had her objective clearly in mind — she wanted to get back to Kansas. With the help of the Scarecrow, the Tin Woodman and the Cowardly Lion, and after many adventures, she was successful. But going home was always her primary consideration. Without a goal, Dorothy would have had no

plan of action and could have remained in the land of Oz forever. The process of Goal Setting involves two steps: Brainstorming and Clarification.

## BRAINSTORMING

The first step in setting goals is to make a list of them. On a blank piece of paper, list all the things you want to achieve in your lifetime. Allow yourself three minutes and be totally uncritical of any goal you may list, even if it appears beyond your abilities, or frivolous. Quickly jot down any goal that comes to mind; you will evaluate them later in the Goal Clarification exercise. Repeat the process for the coming year, and finally for the next month.

## GOAL CLARIFICATION

After making your lists, go back and evaluate each goal. Obviously, the goals you have listed are not equally important. In the Goal Clarification exercise you identify priorities: put first things first. Some goals may be highly desirable, but upon closer examination, you may discover that the goal requires too much of a sacrifice. For instance, many people consider a job promotion highly desirable but may be unwilling to move their family, leave their friends and communities to obtain that goal. Goals often conflict when a major decision has to be made. Eliminate from your list any goal that would require a sacrifice you would be unwilling to make. The purpose of the Goal Clarification exercise is to assist you in making decisions regarding your priorities.

## INSTRUCTIONS FOR THE GOAL CLARIFICATION WORKSHEET

1. On a 1-10 scale, rank each personal preference by asking yourself, 'How important or valuable is this to me?' Record your answer in the Evaluation Column.
2. Make copies of the worksheet so that you have a separate sheet for each goal.
3. Again on a scale of 1-10, rank each of your lifetime, one-year, and one-month goals by asking yourself, 'How much will this goal satisfy my personal preference for...?' Record your answer in the Goal Rank Column.
4. Multiply the evaluation column by the goal rank column for each

preference heading. Record your answers in the Sub-total Column.

5. Add all of your sub-totals and put the sum in the Sum Total blank. The goals with the highest sum totals are your primary goals.

## GOALS CLARIFICATION WORKSHEET

| PERSONAL PREFERENCE | 1-10 EVALUATION | 1-10 GOAL RANK | 1-10 SUB TOTAL |
|---|---|---|---|
| ACCOMPLISHMENT | | | |
| CHALLENGING EXPERIENCE | | | |
| CONTROL | | | |
| CREATIVE EXPRESSION | | | |
| EDUCATION | | | |
| FAME | | | |
| FRIENDSHIP | | | |
| HAPPINESS | | | |
| HELPING OTHERS | | | |
| INDEPENDENCE | | | |
| INNER PEACE | | | |
| LOVE | | | |
| LOYALTY | | | |
| OBEY THE LAW | | | |
| PERSONAL DEVELOPMENT | | | |
| PRODUCTIVITY | | | |
| PROMOTIONS | | | |
| RELIGION | | | |
| RESPECT | | | |
| SELF-RESPECT | | | |
| TEAMWORK | | | |
| WEALTH | | | |
| WHERE YOU LIVE | | | |
| WINNING | | | |
| SUM TOTAL | | | |

## PRIMARY GOAL WORKSHEET

List your top two lifetime, one-year and one-month goals on the primary goal worksheet. These primary goals are the most important for your success and happiness. You may want to post this sheet on your bulletin board or frame it and place in a prominent place. Goals that are visible get accomplished.

## PRIMARY GOAL WORKSHEET

### LIFETIME

_____

_____

_____

_____

_____

_____

### ONE YEAR

_____

_____

_____

_____

_____

### ONE MONTH

_____

_____

_____

_____

_____

## TIME INVENTORY INSTRUCTIONS

Now that you have identified your primary goals, you need to organize your time. Recording and analyzing your activities for the next week will give you an in-depth perspective on how you use your day. This will help you arrange your time to implement your goals.

For this exercise, divide your day into these three segments:
1. From waking until lunch
2. Lunch until dinner
3. After dinner until retiring

At the end of each segment (after lunch, after dinner, in bed just before sleep) write down every activity in which you engaged, noting the amount of time consumed by each one.

Next, group them into broad categories: a) low priority work, b) phone calls, c) socializing, d) meetings, e) personal care (eating, dressing, bathing, etc.) f) television and g) productive work. Write down the amount of time spent on each. Take note of where your time is being spent. The one-day example of Nick's time inventory on the following page may serve as a guideline.

## TIME INVENTORY INSTRUCTIONS
Example of Nick's Time Inventory for one day.

| ACTIVITY | TIME |
|---|---|
| (Waking Until Lunch) | |
| Lying in bed trying to get up | 20 min |
| Shower | 15 min |
| Dress for work | 20 min |
| Eat breakfast | 15 min |
| Commute | 45 min |
| Drop-in visitor | 25 min |
| Low priority work | 60 min |
| Meeting | 50 min |
| Productive work | 60 min |
| (Lunch Through Dinner) | |
| Eat lunch | 60 min |
| Productive work | 25 min |
| Phone | 25 min |
| Low Priority work | 60 min |
| Phone | 20 min |
| Low Priority work | 55 min |
| Daydreaming | 20 min |
| Socializing | 25 min |
| Commute | 45 min |
| Phone | 10 min |
| Phone | 15 min |

| | |
|---|---|
| Neighbor visit | 25 min |
| Eat dinner | 30 min |

(After Dinner to Retiring)

| | |
|---|---|
| Television | 3 hrs |
| Talk to wife | 20 min |
| Help child with homework | 30 min |

| CATEGORICAL LISTING | TOTAL TIME |
|---|---|
| Television | 3 hrs |
| Personal Care | 2 hrs 40 min |
| Low priority work | 2 hrs 55 min |
| Commuting | 1 hr 30 min |
| Productive work | 1 hr 15 min |
| Socializing | 1 hr 15 min |
| Phone | 1 hr 10 min |
| Meeting | 1 hr |

## TIME INVENTORY ANALYSIS

When you analyze your time inventory, be alert for time wasters such as drop-in visitors. Interpersonal relationships are important in the business world, but frivolous friendliness consumes time which could be better spent in more productive endeavors.

The telephone expedites business transactions, but it can also constantly interrupt the normal flow of business. In Nick's case, phone calls meant talking about the weather, sports and other topics unrelated to work. He was able to cut his telephone conversation time in half by circumventing extraneous talk. He began answering the phone by saying, 'Hello, this is Nick. What can I do for you?'

Opening and reading mail can also mean wasted time. If you receive reports you don't need or lots of business magazines and junk mail, then you probably spend a lot of time reading useless data. Take your name off distribution lists, and discard junk mail. Learn to scan the table of contents of business magazines for the more pertinent articles. It is estimated that the average executive spends three months of every working year reading. A speed reading course can double your reading rate, increase your comprehension, and possibly add an extra month-and-a-half's time to your working year. Learn to analyze charts and graphs in magazine articles and skim articles without illustrations. This technique allows some people to cover 1000 words per minute and comprehend the gist of what they have read. Getting through reading material quickly allows you more time to pursue your primary goals.

In addition, failing to delegate properly is a significant time waster. If a task requires only five minutes, you may decide that you can perform the task more quickly and efficiently than anyone else. The problem with this logic is that the five-minute task you do today is the same five-minute task you may have to do tomorrow and the next day, so that by the end of the week, you have spent 25 minutes on this task. By taking the time to properly delegate, you create more time in your work week.

A major reason that people fail to climb past the implementation rung on the wisdom ladder is procrastination. Symptoms of procrastination include daydreaming, rationalizing, inviting interruptions and avoiding tasks that create anxiety. Most people procrastinate because they are afraid of making mistakes or they lack confidence. Procrastinators need to set priorities and deadlines, do one thing at a time, and tackle more difficult problems before doing easier or more pleasant tasks. If you find yourself paralyzed by fear of a project, then break it down into its component parts and work on one part at a time.

Implementation is further enhanced by making a 'to do' list, either at the end of the day or first thing in the morning. Keep your primary goals in mind when scheduling activities and specifically designate the time the task will be completed.

Your list should allow enough flexibility for the unexpected; remember, you can't control every hour. Keep your 'to do' list visible on your desk, dashboard of your car or on your dresser so that it serves as a constant reminder.

If you can't say 'no', you will accept tasks that are not related to your primary goals. If a co-worker asks you for help when your deadlines are drawing near and you say 'yes', then you probably lack the courage required to say 'no'. This subject will be detailed in chapter 3.

Trying to do too much at once, unrealistic planning and impulsive decisions are common maladies of our hurried world. Satellite communications, computers and supersonic jets increase the pace of business life. In seminars, I ask people to raise their hands if they feel there is enough time for normal business activities. So far, not one hand has been raised. Apparently, most of us harbor a sense of urgency and an underlying hostility toward anyone or anything that gets in our way. Good time management — setting goals and priorities, planning, keeping daily 'to do' lists — can help alleviate this problem.

With good time management you will be able to find a segment of time to work toward your primary goals.

## HOW TO LEARN AND STUDY

Confucius said, 'Study as if you were never to master it; as if in fear of losing it.'

In order to study effectively, one must first organize one's schedule so that an uninterrupted quantum of time is created.

Everyone has energy fluctuations and your study time should be during a period when you feel mentally alert and physically refreshed. Analyze your patterns of mental energy and fatigue and schedule your periods of study when your energy level is on an upswing.

The material that you study should be directly related to the attainment of knowledge that will help you achieve a primary goal. Analyze your knowledge requirement and break it down into small segments. Each segment should be attainable within a single study session.

Be sure to define segments that you can finish because a lack of success will discourage you. After a study session, give yourself a reward, such as a snack, movie, or reading a book for pleasure. Rewards are important to reinforce your study behavior.

Keep your study area organized and easily accessible. If your study area gets messy, you will tend to avoid it. It is aggravating and time-consuming to have books and papers scattered all over so that you cannot readily find what you need. Create an indexed filing system for loose papers and a shelving system for books.

When you purposely read a book or article for primary goal attainment, concentrate on what you are reading. The worst way to read a book is to read without reflection. There are four steps for successful reading:

1. Scan each chapter by reading the headings and subheadings. This will give you an overview of the chapter's content and order.
2. Read and thoroughly understand each section before going on to the next section. The main reason people give up, become confused and unable to learn, is because they have gone past a word or section that was not fully understood. Don't go on until you have thoroughly understood what you have previously read. Find the misunderstood word or section and make a renewed effort toward comprehension.
3. Question yourself about the content after reading each section. Write the questions down and mentally answer them. This assures active involvement in reading. Mind wandering will be minimized and comprehension will increase. If you are studying in preparation for an exam, use this record to quiz yourself.

4. After each chapter, review your written questions and mark those that seem most important. The purpose of this final step is to help you think more about the chapter content and to further process the information. Another benefit is that in order to decide which questions are important, one must review the entire chapter.

## THE FINAL RUNG — JUDGEMENT

After repeated climbs up the first five rungs of the wisdom ladder, you are ready for the sixth rung — sound judgement.

DEFINING THE PROBLEM. Correctly defining the problem is of critical importance to the final outcome of the judgmental process. The well formulated problem statement is the focal point that allows and even forces clarity in the later steps of the judgmental process. Oversimplified or inexact problem statements may lead to incorrect answers. The initial question should be carefully examined, expanded and reformulated as necessary.

IDENTIFYING THE ALTERNATIVES. In this stage, reassemble information you have learned and choose the alternatives which seem best adapted to satisfying the problem statement. During study, one brings order to incomplete and often chaotic information. One must then generate a range of possible alternative solutions to the question that has been posed.

CONSIDER THE CONSEQUENCES. Project the possible consequences of implementing each alternative that has been identified. The scope of one's learning, studying and experience plays a critical role in the judgmental process. Consider how the implementation of each particular alternative will affect each person involved.

JUDGEMENT — SELECTING THE BEST ALTERNATIVE. One must rank the most advantageous alternatives then choose the one that best answers the original question. Once the judgment has been made, implement your decision. Without implementation nothing will result.

ANALYZE THE RESULTS. After implementation, one should carefully analyze the results. Through analysis more is gained from the experience. When a similar problem or question arises, future judgmental processes will be easier, quicker, and more accurate. Diligence and careful attention to results enhance experience.

# CLIMBING THE WISDOM LADDER

In every decision we make, we must choose among possible alternatives and determine which alternative best suits our purpose. The more you learn, study and experience a problem or question, the sharper your judgement becomes. Remember, the capacity to become wiser and to make better judgements lies within all of us if we continuously climb the wisdom ladder.

# NICE GUYS DON'T
# FINISH LAST

*In what way should a person in authority act in order to conduct affairs properly? When the person in authority is benevolent without great expenditure; when he lays tasks onto people without their repining; when he pursues what he desires without being covetous; when he maintains a dignified ease without being proud; when he is imposing without being fierce.*

Confucius


*'I have come for my heart,' said the Tin Woodman.*

*'Very well,' said Oz, and brought a pair of tinners' shears and cut a small hole in the left side of the Tin Woodman's breast. Then going through a chest of drawers, he took out a pretty heart, made entirely of silk and stuffed with sawdust. 'Isn't it a beauty,' Oz said.*

*'It is indeed,' replied the Tin Woodman who was greatly pleased. Oz put the heart in the Tin Woodman's chest.*

*'There,' said Oz, 'now you have a heart that any man might be proud of.'*

**The Wizard of Oz**
**L. Frank Baum**

Wishing others well indicates concern for the welfare of others and is a uniquely human behavior. Confucius described benevolent behavior in writing: 'Do not impose on others what you yourself do not desire. Discover what others do or do not want done to them.' The Golden Rule, 'Do unto others as you would have them do unto you,' is identical to Confucius' thoughts. In the self-centered world of the 'Me Generation', courtesy, politeness and respect for the rights of others are often subordinated by self-interest. Truly benevolent people recognize the worth of others and are most willing to openly express warmth, friendliness and consideration to others. To develop benevolence, you must be convinced that being kind and considerate is the best way to conduct yourself in business and in life.

Nice guys don't finish last. Mean-spirited, callous, unfeeling people, who are nonetheless qualified and have excellent work skills, are often passed over for promotion. It is not uncommon to hear this about a candidate for promotion: 'I don't care how intelligent he is, I don't want a human computer; I want someone who gets along with people.' A frown, a sour face, or a stern, unyielding countenance invites fear and creates disunity within an organization. Benevolent people, on the other hand, look compassionately upon fellow workers and thus encourages loyalty and cooperation.

The importance of benevolence cannot be over emphasized. B types listen more than they converse, refrain from harsh words, and speak pleasantly. Benevolent people are empathetic and help others who are troubled. Recognizing and rewarding the accomplishments of others require benevolence. Generous, good hearted, charitable, well-wishing and loving are adjectives that describe a benevolent person.

Some believe that acting with benevolence indicates weakness, irresolution or a 'soft touch'; but a closer look at some adjectives that describe the opposite of benevolence: cruel, mean-spirited, inhuman, malicious, spiteful, stingy, callous, insensitive, unconcerned, unfeeling and malevolent, obviously do not describe desirable characteristics in a leader or manager.

Benevolence must be tempered with wisdom for, as Confucius said, 'To love benevolence without loving learning is bound to lead to foolishness.' The quintessential example of benevolence is Jesus Christ as he was dying on the cross. After being mocked, beaten, crowned with thorns, nailed to a cross and stabbed in the side with a lance, Jesus forgave his tormentors.

Dr Mark Silber of United States International University in San Diego, advocates 'tough love' and the 'four S' formula for managers: sensitivity, structure, style and sincerity. Recently, Joseph A. Kordick, head of the Ford Motor Company Parts and Service Division, said at a meeting of managers, 'I am desperately trying to get my managers to add one dimension to the way they live. I want them to trust and respect. I want them to love and understand. I want them to know what this means and what it can do for us as an organization and for the people we are trying to take care of.' Kordick is aware that unbenevolent managers elicit anger, resentment, dislike of work and lower productivity, while benevolent managers obtain cooperation from employees.

## THE PAYOFF

Whether benevolence is expressed by a friendly or more personal salutation, a tangible approval (i.e. promotion or raise), recognizing the worth of fellow workers, or rewarding productive behavior is indispensible in business and life.

Cynics may see no reward in benevolence, but acts of kindness reap their own rewards. In business, the benevolent manager is rewarded by employees who are loyal, hardworking and more productive. Confucius said it best: 'Moral examples are more effective than edicts. If the leader is good, the followers will be good and will follow the example.' It is true that benevolent leadership encourages superior performance.

## THE BENEVOLENCE PRINCIPLE

When you act benevolently towards others in business, two positive things happen. First, people will cooperate and return your benevolence, thereby enhancing the probability of your success. Secondly, acting benevolently will make you feel good, thereby increasing your effectiveness. Everyone profits from a benevolent interchange. It seems unfortunate that many business people never grasp the 'benevolent principle.'

## THE BENEVOLENT MANAGER

A benevolent manager rewards employees for productive efforts. The chances of an employee behaving according to his manager's wishes are enhanced if the employee knows he will be rewarded. To be most effective, the reward should immediately follow after the desired behavior.

An 'atta boy,' a simple pat on the back, a sincere compliment spoken face to face or by telephone, a short note or memorandum, or an acknowledgement of superior performance posted on the bulletin board are common forms of benevolent reinforcement. Such acknowledgement costs little but is a powerful way to have a job done well. The employee benefits and so does the company!

Benevolent managers recognize people as their most valuable resources. Confucius understood this. When his stables were burned down, he asked, 'Was anyone hurt?' He did not ask about the horses.

The productivity of an organization depends more on the workers than on any other resource. It is costlier to an organization to replace a person than to replace a machine. It is costlier to replace a highly skilled worker than it is to replace the tools. In our technological age, however, there is apparent difficulty in understanding and dealing with the human elements of supervision.

This problem is further pronounced when the supervisor has a scientific or technical background. These people place a premium on precision and control and expect employees to work with great predictability. Such demands can often lead to a conflict. People are not machines and do not appreciate being treated as such. In conclusion, it is essential to be more concerned for people rather than machines.

## A CASE HISTORY

The image of the hardnosed businessman barking orders at subordinates while making decisions with extreme self-confidence is not the norm for successful executives. An effective executive recognizes the need to appreciate and stimulate the abilities of those around him. The manager who demonstrates respect for others and their opinions and suggestions, and at the same time encourages participation in decision-making will have the most productive employees. In the following case study, we will see what happens when a manager neglects these principles.

### Archie

Archie received his MBA ten years ago and went to work in the manufacturing division of a large corporation. Archie was married with no children and was considered aloof by some; hard-driving by others. He was always punctual and seemed interested in his work.

Every morning, Archie would walk down the halls, poke his head into the offices of subordinates, and ask about the progress of various projects. When subordinates attempted to explain project delays, Archie's usual response was, 'Don't tell me about the storms, just bring in the ship!' Archie would then enter the plant to check for inefficient manufacturing processes.

On one tour, he observed that turning a machine on and off required three different steps. Archie concluded that by leaving the machine on, a machinist could save several minutes each time he performed a certain task. By counting the number of times this task was performed, Archie determined that a machinist could save 30 minutes per day or two and one-half hours per week, simply by leaving his machine on. Since the plant employed 20 machinists, Archie was able to save 50 man hours per week by changing this one procedure.

Archie didn't like to waste time on committee meetings. To Archie, meetings were only tools for gathering information in order to make decisions. When Archie held a meeting, he would hand out a written agenda, issue assignments, allow little discussion, and wrap up the meeting after about 15 minutes.

During Archie's first year of management, productivity figures increased rapidly. The first quarter of his second year was a different story. Employee turnover and absenteeism had risen alarmingly. When several key people on his staff resigned, Archie began to suffer from lack of information and found decision-making difficult. Frustrated by this void of information, he began to make impulsive decisions with poor results.

At the end of Archie's second year, union contracts came due for renegotiation. Because productivity had slipped during the past six months, Archie was determined to cut benefits and freeze wages. In a formal presentation to union representatives, he presented facts and figures supporting his recommendations. The union balked at his suggestions and went on strike for several months. During negotiations, employees expressed resentment toward many of Archie's productivity 'improvements'. For example, the noise created by their constantly running machines had made it impossible for the machinists to talk to one another.

Archie did not even have the support of his direct subordinates. When he asked his management team to work toward company goals, he found them lacking both loyalty and commitment. Loyalty was missing because Archie had treated his employees as if they were robots. Commitment was lacking because he had never involved subordinates in the challenges of production or the decision-making process.

Eventually Archie's most talented employees quit or requested transfers. Those who remained were merely order-takers. One day corporate headquarters called Archie in from his manufacturing division and assigned him to a desk job in the main office. This new position involved little responsibility or authority requiring only the generation of statistical information for various company reports.

Six months later, Archie was unhappy enough to seek counseling.

During counseling, Archie revealed that in addition to experiencing difficulties at work, he was also estranged from his wife. He was a lonely man with no friends and few pleasures. Archie conducted personal relationships on an intellectual plane, with little emotional warmth, and a sense of detachment. Simple social graces such as politeness seemed to elude Archie, a man who viewed the world in a coldly logical manner and exhibited little patience with small talk.

When Archie took the WBC-Q, it disclosed that he had a high level of wisdom and courage but had a very low level of benevolence. Archie fits the WC profile of the overly serious, rigid, stubborn person. He neither noticed nor understood the feelings and opinions of others. Decisions were based on facts and the need to get the job done. Little, if any attention was given to the effects his decisions would have on his employees. Archie was overly forceful in his efforts to bend others to his will. Preferring work, Archie was not interested in social events, family gatherings or in pleasing others.

At home, Archie had an undemonstrative relationship with his wife, and dealt with her in cold, analytical terms. Each evening, Archie presented his wife with a list of things to be completed the following day. He made certain demands, such as having dinner served promptly at 6:30, scheduling outings well in advance and having a freshly starched and ironed shirt prepared for him every morning. After attending an assertiveness seminar, his wife realized she didn't enjoy being ordered around and left Archie. He then hired a maid and noticed little difference in his daily routine. However, he did perceive that certain comforts of home were lacking, and realized his personal as well as his professional life was void of meaning.

In discussing his management philosophy, Archie said he considered fear to be a great management tool. 'That means telling people what I want and to get production up or else!' he stated. But Archie discovered that fear, a prime motivator a century ago, had lost much of its punch. Today, most middle managers are motivated by challenge, autonomy and responsibility. In the case of blue collar workers, unions and the unemployment system had blunted the clout of fear as a motivator. As a result, Archie was unable to motivate either segment of his workforce.

Not surprisingly, Archie also complained that people who reported to him were unassertive in their job performance. Subjected to almost daily browbeatings, his employees became demoralized and exhibited little self-confidence. His highly autocratic methods of management had not created a climate for self-confidence to thrive.

**Solutions**
During counseling sessions, it become apparent that Archie had an inaccurate concept of his managerial abilities. He viewed himself as a topnotch manager: able to get the job done in the most logical, efficient way. He had little insight into the opinions, beliefs or motivations of himself or others. Archie was given a series of exercises designed to enhance a sense of benevolence.

One of Archie's major deficits was his poor listening habits. He was astute in listening for factual information, but emotional content largely escaped him. Through training in listening for emotion as well as fact, Archie was able to overcome his problem. Also introduced was an exercise in giving compliments sincerely.

First, a baseline was established to determine how often he gave compliments. Archie rarely complimented anyone for a job well done. A non-committal grunt, or absence of fault-finding was Archie's versions of a compliment. He liked playing the Tough Guy; smiling infrequently and seeming hard to impress. When asked why he rarely gave compliments, he said, 'If I'm too liberal with praise and recognition, I might give someone an exaggerated idea of his value. He might even turn around and ask for a raise.' Archie admitted that he felt somewhat jealous when a subordinate did an outstanding job, as if any recognition extended to others might detract from his own accomplishments.

The importance of recognizing accomplishment was emphasized. Archie realized when employees knew they would get personal credit for their suggestions and that their boss wasn't afraid to let them bask in the limelight, they performed better. Everyone craves compliments and recognition for their work. Several surveys indicate that workers who receive adequate incomes usually value recognition above money.

With his newfound awareness, Archie decided to give more compliments and recognition. Again, a record was kept. At first, Archie found this an arduous and awkward task. However, after several weeks, this behavior became easier and more natural for him. Eventually, Archie was able to significantly increase his rate of giving compliments and recognition.

Archie also needed to improve his written communications. Like his oral communications, his memos were blunt, to the point and tactless. Archie was encouraged to imagine the recipient's response to his memos. This made him soften his writing style. With practice, words such as please and thank you, and closings such as 'My best regards' instead of his usual 'Sincerely', became second nature.

One of the simplest, yet most significant changes involved Archie's use of the phone. In the past, Archie had greeted all callers with a gruff 'Yea?' Not surprisingly, callers found this discourteous, abrupt and abrasive. At the onset of each call, a breeding ground for conflict had been sown. Archie began to answer his phone with, 'Hello, this is Archie, how can I help you?' This greeting was predictably more acceptable to callers and created a more caring relationship at the beginning of each conversation.

The hardest change for Archie involved disciplining subordinates. When his employees made a mistake, Archie felt that it was his job to chew them out in a manner which they would not soon forget, no matter who was within earshot. Often, his tirades were conducted at top volume and punctuated by profanity. On two such occasions, workers had walked off their jobs and out the door. (Archie obviously needed to utilize the seven steps of the Benevolent Discipline Exercise, outlined later in this chapter.)

After extensive role play involving specific, potentially problematic situations, Archie was able to assimilate this disciplinary technique into his everyday management practice.

**Different Man, Different World**
By practicing benevolence, Archie realized he could cause others to act similarly toward him. His perception of the world as a cold, harsh, hostile place began to change. Emerging into a world of potential warmth and humanity, Archie found new meanings for friendship, caring and love. His newfound benevolence on the job carried over into his personal life. He was able to re-establish communication with his wife, and with the help of a marriage counselor, to rebuild his marriage.

A year later, Archie was given the chance to manage a manufacturing division in another city. His wife relocated with him and his career potential is greater than ever.

**BENEVOLENCE REINFORCERS**
The following exercise breathes life into the 'Benevolent Principle'. Most managers overestimate their own benevolence. Therefore, the first step in increasing benevolence in business involves an assessment of benevolence through the WBC-Questionnaire. A low B score indicates a need for improvement. Managers should calculate their own frequency of benevolent actions. Once a

baseline has been determined, a deliberate attempt to increase appropriate expressions of benevolence toward employees should be made. Initially, it may seem unnatural or even staged, but all new behavior feels awkward at first. The responses of those being complimented or rewarded will reassure the manager.

The steps toward increasing benevolent behavior are:

1. Become aware of your benevolence by taking the WBC-Q.
2. Record your daily reward and reinforcement rate to determine a baseline.
3. Increase your baseline by deliberately increasing the number of 'positive strokes' (verbal reinforcements) you give to others.
4. Continue to keep a daily tally of your reinforcement rate to increase your awareness of the number of times your employees do things to your satisfaction. Remember things that get rewarded get done!

Managers who are problem solvers, accustomed to giving orders only when things go wrong, may remain silent when things go well. It will require extra effort to praise people for work well done, but the payoff makes it worthwhile. Benevolent management yields higher employee morale, higher management morale, and ultimately, increased productivity.

## Benevolent Criticism

Benevolent managers don't disregard poor performance. Every manager must eliminate mistakes and sub-standard work. It is a delicate matter when a manager corrects a subordinate, especially when the employee has invested time, effort and emotion into a project. Even though employees may tolerate constructive criticism, the process is still uncomfortable and often painful.

How can a manager be benevolent and still criticize and correct poor performances? A benevolent manager does not begin a confrontation with criticism. Critical opening statements put people on the defensive; and defensive people do not listen.

The best way to correct an employee is to praise the worker but criticize the work. Sandwich criticism between praise. For example, start the discussion by pointing out what the employee is doing right and praising that aspect of their work. Next, gently shift the focus of the discussion to the area which needs correction. Calmly suggest a better way to do the task. End the conversation with a friendly word, a pat on the back or some other signal which indicates that the employee is still a respected member of the team. The 'sandwich technique' leaves the employee with a better understanding of the problem and a feeling that he has not been chastised but helped.

When managers criticize without benevolence, employees may become maliciously obedient. Employees will precisely obey an order even though in the future, circumstances may change so that a different approach is warranted. 'If that good for nothing supervisor wants me to do it his way,' the maliciously obedient employee thinks, 'then that's the way I'll do it, even though I know it's wrong. He will learn soon enough.'

### Benevolent Discipline

Discipline denotes both punishment and teaching. When the two are mixed, the result is benevolent discipline, an enlightened but firm philosophy for dealing with problem employees. Benevolent discipline requires active listening and an accurate interpretation of facial gestures, body language, tone of voice and vocal inflections. These clue the manager into the underlying motivation of the employee. When differences exist between verbal and non-verbal messages, the non-verbal communication usually expresses the truth. For example, if an employee says, 'I like my job,' but does so in a flat, unenthusiastic vocal expression, with averted eyes and nervous gestures, he may be, in truth, feeling the opposite. In contrast, an employee who states, 'I like my job,' in a positive, energetic tone of voice, with direct eye contact, and a firm confident stance, can be believed.

Once the message is understood, the other half of the communication process is to let an employee know that his feelings and point of view have been heard. To the employee who unconvincingly states, 'I like my job,' the manager might say, 'I know that you do not like all aspects of your job, but what can I do to make things better?' Confirming non-verbal messages opens up communication and allows an honest interchange of ideas.

Benevolent discipline allows employees to retain their self-respect. Employees lose face when they are reprimanded publicly.

This often happens when managers become exasperated and angrily criticize an employee in front of co-workers. Such confrontations are always counter-productive. The employee may quit, cause a scene, or become passive-aggressive and maliciously obedient. A good rule of thumb is to praise in public, discipline in private. Productive discussions are made possible when employees are allowed self respect. What follows are the steps involved in benevolent discipline.

Guidelines for Benevolent Discipline:

1. Describe to the employee the specific problem.
2. Describe your expected standard.
3. Ask the employee to identify what he believes to be the cause of the problem.
4. Ask for his suggestions to solve the problem, and discuss them.
5. Decide on a plan to improve performance.
6. Follow up.
7. Feedback.

Suppose you are the manager of a company and have noticed that an employee's tardiness has become a major problem. As a manager, you have kept records that indicate this employee is coming to work 15 to 30 minutes late, two to five times a week. How do you address the problem?

First, describe the specific problem by meeting with the employee and reviewing the written record concerning his tardiness. Be careful not to generalize, for this makes employees defensive and they will stop listening. For example, if you say, 'You are always coming in late to work,' the subordinate knows he is not always late and thus discounts the criticism as unfair and untrue.

In step two, describe the expected standard. For example, Arrive at work promptly at 9 am. Make allowances for unexpected emergencies. If for some reason, you cannot be on time, call and let me know.' Sometimes an employee may think that coming in late is normal, and has no idea that tardiness is unacceptable, especially if a number of people in the organization are habitually late.

In step three, the employee is asked to identify the cause of the problem. Many managers mistakenly assume that they know the cause of the problem, and fail to ask the employee questions. In regard to tardiness, the idea that an employee is lazy, doesn't care about work, oversleeps, or can't manage time may be inaccurate. Discover the employee's conception of a problem before you make conclusions.

Step four, soliciting the employee's suggestions and solutions, is critical. Once employees begin to look at solutions to a problem, they begin to assume ownership of both the problem and the solution. As a manager, you may want to make a list of solutions to discuss individually or to be copied and given to the employee to serve as a reminder.

Step five requires a decision and an agreement on a course of action. The final decision should be clear and unambiguous. Avoid solutions stated in vague or general terms. In regard to tardiness, simple solutions such as getting more sleep or getting up earlier may be all that is necessary. If given enough thought, even complex problems can be solved easily.

Step six, follow up, is often overlooked by managers. If this step is omitted, an agreement will usually fall apart. In the case of tardiness, a written record should be kept over a period of several weeks with the employee's knowledge and consent.

Step seven involves feedback to employees regarding progress. Few people change established patterns of behavior quickly. In the example of tardiness, if the rate has been reduced from three times a week to once a week, the employee should be complimented. The ultimate goal may not have been reached, but progress is evident. Continued use of benevolent discipline will assure further improvement. At first, the manager must reinforce all improvements; but after a while, rewards may be delayed and intermittent. Eventually, the employee will be routinely punctual and will not require constant supervision from the manager.

## Benevolent Discipline — Role Play Exercise

Think of a specific personnel problem that you have within your organization and write it down in detail. Next, write down the answers to the following questions:

1. What is the usual standard of performance?
2. How is the employee performing?
3. What do you think the employee will say is the cause of the problem?

4. What action do you think will resolve the problem?

Ask a friend to role play a benevolent discipline exercise with you acting as the problem employee and your friend playing the manager. By placing yourself in the employee's shoes, you may gain insight into how the employee perceives the problem. Your friend, in the role of manager, must be authoritarian. As you, the employee, grapple with the inflexibility of the manager, your own solutions to the problem will come into focus. Refer to the first five steps of benevolent discipline (page 62). By practicing the various steps of benevolent discipline with a friend you will be prepared to deal more effectively with the situation in real life. The role reversal allows you to show more empathy toward your employee's predicament. Follow up and feedback, of course, should not be forgotten.

### Benevolent Listening

Learning to listen requires more training than learning to read or speak. Clergyman, psychiatrists, psychologists and social workers know the importance of benevolent listening. People innately like to talk more than they like to listen. All of us have had the experience of speaking to someone who is not really listening. Restlessness, nervousness and most of all, roving eyes, communicate inattentiveness. How often in conversation do you not listen but rather formulate your own ideas, waiting to interject them at the next pause? A friend who worked in a factory once spoke of many production procedures that were inefficient. Several times, he made suggestions to his foreman about better ways to do the job. Impatience and eyes glazed with disinterest greeted his suggestions, so that eventually he made no more attempts. The foreman was an inactive, non-benevolent listener.

It is an axiom that benevolent people and effective managers listen more than they speak. Developing benevolent listening requires thought and concentration. As the manager listens to an employee, judgements must be made. Is this information important? Does it need further refinement?

Managers who seek an employee's solutions to problems, and who listen benevolently, are exhibiting respect. Respect is a benevolent characteristic usually activated by someone of superior learning, achievement, character and generosity. Once an employee makes viable recommendations, the manager must support the employee's solutions. If the employee's recommendations are ignored in favor of the manager's 'best solution', future suggestions are discouraged. Do not ask employees for solutions if you have already made up your mind.

Over the phone we rely on tone of voice and choice of words to convey a message. Because we can't see one another, non-verbal communication — the most powerful means of communicating a message — is absent. Tone of voice can express benevolence, neutrality or malice. When you are harried, hurried or harrassed, irritability edges into your tone of voice. When a telephone communication begins with one person displaying irritation or anger, the tendency is for the other to react similarly or to end the call as quickly as possible. Another annoying response is a tone of voice which indicates, 'I am a busy person. I have no time for you.'

One has the option of answering the phone in a pleasant and friendly way, in a non-caring manner, or in a gruff, unfriendly and hostile voice. Common sense tells us that benevolent telephone communications are best. A firm, friendly tone which projects interest in the caller, together with kind words that invite a response comprise benevolent telephone communication. Why, then, don't more people act that way? The answer is simple. Most people don't know that they are communicating non-benevolently.

For example, Sam, a customer service manager, felt that the demands on his time interfered with the conduct of routine business. Sam especially complained that the telephone wasted too much of his time. Sam's attitude caused complaints from customers and he was referred for counseling. The WBC-Q revealed that Sam was low on benevolence, but he insisted this wasn't true. Sam was persuaded to keep a time log of his work day, especially noting time spent on the phone. During the next counseling session, Sam's time log disclosed that he spent two to three hours per day on the telephone. He admitted that much of his time was consumed by lengthy telephone conversations. Without Sam's knowledge, I phoned and tape recorded him. After an assurance that the taped phone conversation was confidential and only for our counseling sessions, I played it back for him. Sam had no idea how he sounded: hostile and rude. He was given the audio tape with the suggestions that he listen to it at his leisure.

To improve his phone communication, Sam was instructed to say as pleasantly as possible, 'Hello, this is Sam, can I help you?' This greeting was practiced several times during the counseling session and later was typed in capital letters and taped to Sam's phone to act as a reminder. It worked!

This simple solution helped Sam develop benevolence both in his tone of voice and choice of words. The payoff for Sam was almost immediate. His telephone conversations became more relaxed and pleasant and his work life more enjoyable. The time he spent on the phone diminished markedly and he was able to complete all his work during the usual course of a business day.

**Benevolence in Written Communication**
In the age of electronic communication, the written word sometimes gets overlooked. Aspiring authors and book lovers appreciate a nicely turned phrase, realizing the time and effort involved in its conception. No one denies the impact of a written performance evaluation, good or bad. Perhaps, as some suggest, writing has gone out of style; but I believe the written word will always be the foundation of human enterprise. All professions require a certain amount of written communication.

A common practice in writing business communications consists of eliminating all unneccessary verbage, using few descriptive adjectives and avoiding all personal references. This results in a stiff and sterile message devoid of warmth and the human touch. Such communications create the impression that the writer is uncaring, distant, cold or blunt. Benevolence in written communication imparts a personal touch appreciated by everyone.

Charles, an ambitious yet sensitive manager, consulted me when his letters were criticized as inappropriate for business communications. Customers complained that Charles' missives were more like missiles.

They felt offended by the short, abrupt notes. Customers felt that Charles didn't understand their needs and threatened to take their business elsewhere. At work, Charles was known for his cool, efficient and pragmatic manner. This was reflected in his dress and his relationships with co-workers. But away from work, Charles was personable, conversed readily, smiled easily and appeared relaxed. This was Charles' real personality.

Charles' WBC-Q was well balanced, but at work his benevolence was inhibited. Charles was essentially a benevolent person masquerading at work as a detached, formal and aloof manager — his concept of the ideal businessman.

Charles was encouraged to be himself, a man whose 'off-duty' personality characteristics were highly desirable in a manager. It was suggested that before writing a letter, Charles go into his office, take off his coat, unbutton his vest and the top button of his shirt, loosen his tie, put his feet on the desk and relax. While dictating the first draft of a letter, he was advised to let the words come spontaneously. At the same time, he was told to visualize the facial expressions and emotional responses of each letter's recipient. Not only were Charles' words more benevolent, he was also pleased by the change in his writing style and surprised that little rewriting was necessary. After repeating the exercise several times, Charles became more relaxed and felt more at ease as his natural warmth and benevolence began to permeate his writing.

## BENEVOLENCE IN PERSPECTIVE

In a civilized society, benevolent interactions are best. This doesn't mean casting off your three-piece suit and donning a saffron robe, nor does it mean continually turning the other cheek. Benevolence, as espoused in this book, refers to attitudes and behaviors which reflect a concern for others. Diplomacy, the art and practice of conducting negotiations and affairs without arousing hostility, comes close to the definition of benevolence.

Benevolence is a behavior anyone can acquire and develop. Confucius admitted that benevolence is difficult to achieve, but he said, 'Whether we accede to benevolence depends solely on ourselves and not on others.' Benevolence implies morality: cultivating a sense of right and wrong. Benevolent people always proceed from the belief that if one does what is right, worries and fears disappear, and ventures will end successfully. Benevolence must be properly mixed with wisdom and courage. The rule of synergy applies to each: the total effect is greater than the sum of the effect made independently. Confucius was aware of the synergistic principle when he said, 'In conducting business, the superior man is anxious that he should be reverently attentive; in retirement to be sedately grave; in intercourse with others to be strictly sincere; when angry, to think of the difficulties anger may bring him; when acquiring a gain, to think of righteousness. Though a man go among rude, uncultivated tribes, these qualities may not be neglected.'

Benevolence in business is beneficial because everyone gains.

## BENEVOLENCE — WHAT'S IN IT FOR YOU?

The cliche, 'What goes around comes around,' is completely accurate when we practice benevolence. The benevolent deeds you do will be reciprocated. When you smile at people they will smile back.

The glorious feeling of benevolence comes closest to a feeling of spirituality and goodness. Without benevolence, we are like the Tin Woodman who thought he could not love. The truly benevolent can see the beauty of the world, feel the warmth of friendship, and understand the complexities of emotions. The goodness of our very souls is expressed through our benevolent thoughts and deeds.

# FROM COWARDICE TO
# COURAGE

'The man of courage pursues his objectives fearlessly. The man of courage is never afraid. Faced with what is right and to have it undone, indicates a lack of courage.'

Confucius

'I have come for my courage,' announced the Cowardly Lion. 'Very well,' answered the Wizard who went to a high shelf, took down a square green bottle, the contents of which he poured into a green-gold dish beautifully carved.

'Drink,' said the Wizard. 'What is it?' asked the Lion. 'Well,' answered Oz, 'If it were inside of you, it would be courage. You know, of course that courage is always inside one so that this really cannot be called courage until you have swallowed it.'

The Lion hesitated no longer but drank until the dish was empty. 'How do you feel now?' asked Oz. 'Full of courage,' replied the Lion who went joyfully back to join his friends and tell them of his good fortune.

The Wizard of Oz
L. Frank Baum

Courage is defined in *Webster's Dictionary* as 'a quality of the mind, or temperament, that enables one to stand fast in the face of opposition, hardship or danger.' Courageous action depends on the situation. In war, violence is redefined as bravery and soldiers destroy property and human beings. For athletes, courage is competition and excelling over others. Courage is often determination and as Henry Kissinger once said, 'In a President, determination is better than intelligence.' Courage in business encompasses all of these definitions — morality, bravery, competition, determination and risk-taking.

Courage is a double-edged sword. Confucius said, 'When applied to the good, it is a means to the realization of goodness. In the hands of the wicked, it is a realization to the means of wickedness. Neither great goodness nor great wickedness can be achieved by a man devoid of courage.'

Courage lies midway between cowardice and recklessness. In business, cowardice means timidity and indecisiveness. Passive people seldom succeed. More obvious, and equally bad, are rudeness, impetuosity and overt hostility. Courage not tempered with wisdom and benevolence often leads to over-zealous, reckless actions and failure to reach goals.

Confucius said that he disliked men who possessed courage, but lacked the spirit of virtue. He said, 'Possessed of courage but devoid of morality, a superior man will make trouble while a small man will be a brigand.'

In business, courageous behavior is assertive behavior. In unknown territory, courage may skew in the direction of recklessness; but, when wisdom is blended with courage, risks are reduced. When someone slows progress in a business negotiation, he must then blend benevolence with courage to win over the uncooperative person to his point of view. The courageous person never loses sight of the goal and marshals wisdom and benevolence in the pursuit of his objectives. Blind courage more often than not misses the mark.

To be really effective, the courageous person first climbs the 'wisdom ladder', analyzes the people involved, and proceeds benevolently toward objectives. The goal must be pursued relentlessly, and may require many courageous trips up the 'wisdom ladder'. Courageous people may not always be liked but are usually respected.

## WISDOM WITHOUT COURAGE

Timid people who possess great wisdom yet fail to apply their learning are inhibited and unassertive because they fear failure and criticism. Hiding indecision behind reams of data, Ws' intellectualization represents cowardly behavior. Decisions are antithetical to Ws who lack courage. They withdraw into a world of concepts and ideas, ignoring tasks that require dealing assertively with people. Passive people, who like Walter Mitty live adventurously only in their minds, lack courage to implement ideas.

## BENEVOLENCE WITHOUT COURAGE

Pure benevolence outside of a cloister may be impractical at best, and cowardly at worst. Unless mixed with courage and wisdom, kindness, generosity and concern for others may hinder accomplishment. When the opinion of others becomes a primary motivating factor, emotions govern decisions. This negates the importance of fact, logic and commitment to the right course of action in decision-making. Benevolent people who lack courage fear rejection.

Passive people confuse aggression with courage. An act of aggression is willful and militant, and specifically intended to hurt or harm others. A courageous act, on the other hand, involves an assertive intention to reach a specific goal. In some minds, courage and aggression are the same; however, this belief can inhibit decision-making and the attainment of goals.

## COURAGE AND FEAR

Anxiety and fear, the companions of cowardice, inhibit courage. Depending on the situation, anxiety or fear may or may not be appropriate responses. In battle, fear is realistic and appropriate and serves an adaptive function: kill or be killed. In civilian life fear and anxiety can be maladaptive. Inappropriate fear lies at the core of cowardice. The most common fears are fear of rejection, fear of criticism, and most of all, fear of failure. Fearing rejection, a person hesitates to displease others. Similarly, one may not act if he is thin-skinned and greatly fears criticism. Linked to fear of criticism is the most deadly fear — the fear of failure. This fear inhibits courage. When a person gives in to these fears, he may be less anxious and feel more comfortable; but he pays a terrible price. Cowards don't reach their goals. They lose self-respect and self-esteem, making it more difficult to be courageous in the future.

## A CASE HISTORY

Five years ago, Marsha received her liberal arts degree from an Ivy League university. She then became employed with a Fortune 500 company as a college recruiter. She was considered an insightful interviewer, able to select the best and brightest from the many graduates she interviewed. Her recruiting trips to college campuses were well thought out in advance. Marsha worked long hours and traveled extensively. She never protested when given assignments that she considered unfair. When the Manager of College Recruiting position became available, Marsha was promoted. This position required directing, motivating and discipling eight subordinates. During Marsha's first few months, the department's morale was exceptionally high and the department's performance was better than ever.

But the honeymoon was soon over, as each of her subordinates started to test Marsha's limits. At first, old work habits prevailed and good workers continued to produce good work. Then, one worker arrived a half hour late for work. Marsha knew about this tardiness but said nothing. During the next few weeks, several other employees were tardy. Still, Marsha said nothing. Soon, employees were coming in late almost every day.

On several occasions, Marsha gave work assignments to remote college campuses. Several subordinates protested, feeling that these assignments were unfair. On other occasions, her subordinates cited personal obligations as reasons for not wanting to accept these assignments. Marsha succumbed to her subordinates' protests and excuses without questioning them.

The major objective of Marsha's college recruiting section was to interview recent college graduates and invite the best for second interviews at the operating divisions. But Marsha had to keep costs down by limiting the number of second interviews. The managers of the operating divisions were normally limited to interviewing five graduates for each vacancy. When these managers pressured Marsha to allow them more second interviews, she relented. As a result, she exceeded her budget.

With one month left in the college recruiting season, Marsha had an overwhelming number of job vacancies left to fill. She thus formed a committee to develop a plan for filling these vacancies. The committee met several hours a day for an entire week, but results of the 75 man hours spent in the committee were negligible. The committee members enjoyed one another's company and developed reams of information, but no firm plan of action.

During her career, Marsha had no difficulty responding to demands made by superiors. Her new manager, however, was demanding and knew little about the college recruiting process. When he told Marsha to do something she considered unnecessary, she responded without protest. When the error became apparent, her manager accepted none of the responsibility. He frequently criticized and browbeat Marsha in the presence of her subordinates. After several of these intimidating sessions, Marsha sought counseling.

## Low on Courage

During the first counseling session, Marsha's non-verbal behavior indicated a lack of courage. She avoided eye contact, kept her eyes down, and when she did look up, tears were in her eyes. She walked in a shuffle, and slumped her shoulders. She shifted her weight from one foot to the other, while wringing her hands. When invited to sit down, Marsha said 'Thanks' in an apologetic tone. During the entire interview, her responses were mumbled and hesitant. She bit her lips and adjusted her clothing. Fillers such as 'uh' and 'you know', and negatives such as 'don't bother' and 'it's not really important' punctuated her speech.

When Marsha took the WBC-Q, it disclosed that she had a high level of wisdom, and a high level of benevolence, but a low level of courage. Marsha fit the BW profile of a kind, generous and amiable person with an ability to plan and analyze information. Many people sought her counsel because of her compassion, understanding and ability to develop logical solutions to problems.

When asked about her home life, Marsha described her husband and three children in glowing, loving terms. But she also proceeded to reveal an underlying hostility toward some of their demands. They expected her to prepare a hot breakfast and dinner, to do the laundry and clean the house. In addition, Marsha was expected to wash the dishes nightly, wash the car and take care of the lawn. With her family content and Marsha concealing her resentment, life appeared grand. But when Marsha was promoted, things began to change. Her husband became surly, made unreasonable demands and drank heavily. As a recruiter, Marsha earned less than her husband. In her new managerial position, however, her salary exceeded her husband's, resulting in his feelings of indequacy. In her managerial position, Marsha had to work long hours and often had to bring work home. She had less time to help her children with their homework. Their grades reflected Marsha's inattention and resulted in one of her three children failing the sixth grade.

The combination of a stressful work life and deteriorating family life created an increasingly difficult burden for Marsha. Headaches, nervousness and bouts of insomnia began to plague her. She began waking with excruciating pain in her jaw, after grinding her teeth in her sleep. She had gained 15 pounds in three months. Prior to assuming her managerial position, Marsha had attended an aerobics class regularly. But increased demands on her time had forced her to drop out.

### Add a Measure of Courage

During counseling, we discussed Marsha's beliefs. Many were acquired during her childhood. She believed that she had to think of others first, to give to others even if she was hurting and to act inferior to others. We worked on these irrational beliefs with the Thought Stopping Exercise, described later in this chapter (see page 79).

Many of the counseling sessions which followed involved role playing exercises for specific situations in which Marsha wanted to become more courageous. We worked on Marsha's non-verbal behavior, videotaping and discussing eye contact, posture, hand gestures and gait. In situation after situation, Marsha became more courageous. Her success in one situation led her to attempt more difficult situations. After a few months, Marsha became more courageous in life.

Today Marsha has her college recruiting section under control. Subordinates no longer try to take advantage of her and her boss treats her with respect.

Marsha's most difficult and anxious moment occurred when she suggested to her husband that they seek marriage counseling. The mere suggestion that something was wrong with their marriage caused him to change his overly demanding behavior toward Marsha. Little by little, she taught her children to become more independent in their schoolwork and to assume more household chores. Adding a good measure of courage to her WBC profile assisted Marsha in achieving a more satisfying, fulfilling life.

## COURAGE AND COGNITIONS

Our thoughts and beliefs determine how we behave. Albert Ellis, author and psychotherapist, has said, 'Our thinking and feelings are directly linked to each other and our behavior follows their lead.' The sequence of behavior is: thinking — feeling — behaving. Thinking is called self-talk: an interior dialogue that influences our feelings and behavioral patterns. Negative thoughts may produce fear and anxiety, resulting in negative behaviors. The important principle is: *Negative self-talk increases fear and anxiety and prevents courageous behavior.*

Irrational beliefs often lead to negative self-talk. For example, if you always need approval from every person you deem significant, you are setting up anxiety-producing, negative self-talk when a situation demands confrontation or disciplinary action. Negative self-talk promotes a reluctance to confront or displease others. The belief that virtually everyone should love you is irrational! Such a belief causes anxiety and contributes to frustration and unhappiness.

The concept of being perfect and never making mistakes spawns fear of failure, which causes anxiety i.e., uncourageous behavior. This irrational belief must be challenged. Failing in one endeavor is not equivalent to being a total failure. Win or lose, experience is gained and will lead to more confidence.

For example, a man doing well at his job may have irrational thoughts that he will be fired. The sequence of thoughts can go: 'If I lose my job, I will have no money... If I have no money, I cannot pay my bills, and my creditors will take everything I own... If I have nothing, my wife will leave me. If my wife leaves...' The anxious thoughts can go on endlessly.

Remember this sequence: thinking — feeling — behaving. If thinking negative thoughts has become a habit, they must be eliminated.

## Thought Stopping Exercise

We have control over what we think. Thought stopping, a well-known behavioral technique, begins with the recognition of irrational thoughts. It is then followed by the command, 'Stop, get out of there,' repeated as many times as necessary to force the thought out of your mind. In a sense, the mind is like a tape recorder that plays back irrational thoughts, each time producing more anxiety. As you become aware of this pernicious process, you can reduce its frequency with thought stopping. The next step is substituting a positive thought for the one which has been stopped. For the man who was fearful of losing his job, more appropriate thoughts include, 'These thoughts are ridiculous. My job is secure. Even if my job is in jeopardy, I can choose other employment opportunities.'

Some people have difficulty with thought stopping and thought substitution. Some thought patterns have existed a lifetime and are difficult to change. If this is the case, the 'ouch technique' can be employed. Put a rubber band around your wrist and snap it when unwanted thoughts come into your mind. The momentary pain will help stop the unwanted thought. This may have to be repeated several times, and although it may sound absurd and simplistic, many people have been helped by this behavioral technique.

Remember, stopping established, irrational thoughts may take a while. The idea is to replace the negative thought with a rational statement. Eventually, such unwanted thoughts will be less and less frequent and, in most cases, will cease altogether. The unwanted thought, like a friend who refuses to leave your house when the party's over, may be difficult to deal with, so be persistent.

FROM COWARDICE TO COURAGE

## Communication Skills and Courage

The criteria for courageous behavior would be easier to describe and emulate if they were more readily observable. These types of human behavior can be observed and quantified to some extent. The first is motor behavior — physical actions, posture, stance, gestures and facial expressions. The second is language or speech. The third is tone of voice. Physical actions, actual speech and tone of voice can communicate every emotional and motivational state.

In his book *Silent Messages*, Dr. Albert Mehrabian divides communication skills into three components: verbals, vocals and non-verbals. Verbals are, of course, the words used to communicate a message and would seem to be the most important. However, accordingly to Dr. Mehrabian, verbals communicate only 7 percent of what we say. The choice of words, type of statement and fluency of speech are all parts of verbal behavior and indicate intelligence, educational background, as well as the desire and intent of a speaker. Vocals, the tone of voice used to convey a message, communicates 38 percent of what we say. The tone may be harsh, moderate, or pleasant. It may be a scream or a whisper. Vocals say more than words. Words can evoke different responses depending on the tone of voice.

For example, if you called a stranger in a bar 'a real brute', a brawl might break out. To a friendly business rival who had successfully concluded a shrewd but somewhat unethical business deal, the identical words spoken in an even tone of voice but with a hint of approbation, might evoke a smile of satisfaction and a free drink. The same phrase, 'You are a real brute,' when cooed into the ear of a man following vigorous lovemaking, would communicate an entirely different message. Non-verbals, physical movements, posture, gestures and facial expressions, Dr. Mehrabian found, communicates 55 percent of what we say.

Non-verbal communications focus on motor movements and are eight times more effective in communication than words and almost twice as effective as tone of voice. It is not so much what you say but how you say it that determines the listener's perception of you.

How would you respond to identical advice from two people with very different non-verbals? One person is fidgety, not looking you in the eye, keeping a hand over his mouth and repeatedly adjusting the collar of his shirt. The other person looks you straight in the eye, makes gestures to emphasize certain points and listens quietly with no unnecessary movements. Obviously, the second person would gain your confidence.

### Courage — Verbals, Vocals and Non-verbals

Courageous people speak succinctly. People with courage speak in simple, declarative sentences or ask short questions. Courageous people make many 'I' statements prefaced by 'I think', 'I feel', 'I believe' and 'I know'. They answer questions decisively and briefly: 'Yes', 'no', 'that's correct', 'I can do it'. In contrast, passive or cowardly people speak in rambling statements, give ambiguous answers and use words which indicate indecision. 'Maybe', 'I wonder if you could', 'perhaps', 'I'm not sure', 'I think so', 'I don't know if it would work'. Fillers such as 'Uhh, well, you know', and repetitious phrases crowd the speech of the uncourageous. Uncertainty permeates the speech of timid people and does not instill confidence or enlist the cooperation of others.

The vocal tone of a courageous person is strong, steady, firm, clear and unwavering. His words are pronounced and enunciated flawlessly. His tone is pleasant and conversational, or strong and commanding, depending on the circumstance. The courageous person emphasizes key words by modulation of tone. Courageous people are often good orators and, like Winston Churchill or Abraham Lincoln, they make lasting impressions with the words they speak.

The vocal tone of a cowardly person is easily recognizable. His voice is edged with fear and his tone unsteady. It may crack and unexpectedly hit a high pitch, waiver, or break up due to anxious, irregular breathing. Not all voices are mellifluous; but the tone of a non-courageous person is immediately recognizable, not because of the lack of resonance but because of the noticeable presence of fear.

The body language of a courageous person commands attention and invites respect. Many politicians, talk-show hosts, and evangelists have mastered courageous posture. Motor movements involve mostly the upper torso, and include gestures of the arms (especially the hands). The torso of the courageous speaker will be slightly inclined toward the listener. Courageous gestures include: hammering home the point (fist hitting open palm of opposite hand), making a point (index finger pointing upwards), and beckoning the audience (both palms up, hands moving rhythmically from the audience to the speaker).

Good actors and successful trial lawyers are masters at non-verbal communication. President Ronald Reagan and Pope John Paul II had acting experience before their respective elevation to the presidency and papacy. Both are marvelous non-verbal communicators and use facial expressions, eye contact and upper body gestures masterfully. The eyes, 'the windows to the soul', powerfully communicate courage and determination. The next time you see evangelist Billy Graham on television, turn off the sound and watch him. Observe his movements and countenance, and see how his face projects the conviction of his beliefs.

The coward's gestures are minimal, and motor movements may include nervous tics or aimless actions. Slouching posture, darting or averted eyes, or a face etched with fear project uncertainty. In extreme cases, a person may be paralyzed with fear or even faint. Cowardly non-verbals can convey the message: 'Don't look to me for leadership.'

### The Development of Courage
Like any skill, courage evolves through practice. Fear and anxiety inhibit courage, but can be surmounted by practicing courageous behavior. Practice can be mental rehearsal, behavior rehearsal or role playing.

Preparation for the three methods is identical. First, identify a real life situation in which you want to be more courageous. You may ressurect one from the past, which you wish you had handled differently. For example, the situation might consist of approaching an important customer, giving a speech or disagreeing with the boss. Identify the person(s) involved, the matter being discussed, and the place where the meeting will occur. Determine which facets of your behavior need improving — verbal, vocal, non-verbal, or all three. And remember the relationship between fear and courage. The greater the fear, the more difficult it is to be courageous.

Therefore, practice the less stressful situations first. A tightrope walker illustrates this principle in practice, as he develops skill by walking on a rope only a foot off the ground and gradually moves the rope higher. As your confidence grows, so does your self-assurance and your individual expression of courage.

### Mental Rehearsal

The most effective way of reducing anxiety in a specific situation is 'systematic desensitization', a technique developed by Dr Joseph Wolpe of Temple University. Dr Wolpe discovered the powerful effect of anxiety on certain behaviors. He found that by systematically visualizing situations of fear in their minds, individuals attenuated anxiety and could express their inhibitions. This technique, subsequently tested by many investigators, proved 90 percent effective in reducing the fears which block certain behaviors. The rationale for using systematic desensitization, or mental rehearsal, is based on the direct relationship of fear to courage. As fear (anxiety) is reduced, courage is more easily increased. By repeatedly imagining the selected scenario, fear is reduced. Imagination prepares us for the real life encounter.

The technique is not difficult. After you select the situation in which you lack courage, go to a quiet place where you will not be disturbed. Get comfortable, and clear your mind by taking at least ten slow, even, deep breaths. Concentrate only on your breathing. Notice the air passing easily and freely in and out of your lungs. Then visualize the scene. If the scene is complicated, record it on an audio cassette and after the tenth breath, listen to the tape and visualize the scene at the same time. After you have thought out the scene, take three deep breaths and relax. Determine which part of the scene needs improvement and how it can be improved. Play back the audio cassette or revisualize the scene, making the changes you desire. Repeat the scene as often as necessary.

Mental rehearsal is a powerful technique for improving courage in real life. This technique has helped people increase courage in communications and even in athletic competition. After you are satisfied that mental rehearsal has lowered your anxiety and fear, you may want to practice behavioral rehearsal and/or role playing before dealing with 'real life' situations.

## Behavioral Rehearsal

Feedback and self-criticism are important in improving verbal, vocal and non-verbal behavior. A full-length mirror and an audio cassette recorder or video recording system can aid your verbal, vocal and non-verbal observations. Stand in front of the mirror or the television camera, activate the video equipment if available, and begin your rehearsal. Initially, you may feel foolish and self-conscious, but this feeling will disappear with practice. Preparation also eliminates fear and leads to a more courageous presentation. President Franklin D. Roosevelt's famous fireside chats and Winston Churchill's stirring radio speeches during World War II seemed spontaneous, but historians tell us they were really well rehearsed. Churchill even had his scripts marked with notations to pause, lower his voice, or emphasize certain passages!

Feedback, in the form of honest self-criticism can improve your performance and confidence. Critique your verbal, vocal and non-verbal behavior and note the changes you feel are needed. Tape your practices in sequence to compare previous attempts with recent ones. Positive changes will encourage a better performance next time.

## Role Playing

Now it is time to practice courage with another person. Ask a trusted friend for assistance and explain your objectives. Ask him or her, to read this section of the book in order to understand your purpose. Since vocals and non-verbals are the most important aspects of courage, tell your friend you want to concentrate specifically on developing these areas. It is easier to role play with a prepared script, but an extemporaneous interchange will give the best results.

Begin a realistic dialogue about the chosen situation. Record the interchange so that you can analyze what you did right and wrong. Pinpoint some specific changes you can make to improve the expression of courage. Repeat the exercise several times with your friend until you become less anxious, less fearful, and more proficient and confident. Eventually, joyful anticipation will replace your anxiety about the 'real life' situations.

## Practice for Courage

Courageous people are not necessarily people who have no fears. Anxiety and fear are emotions that everyone feels occasionally. Courageous people realize that despite all their anxieties and fears, only a small percentage of the negative consequences they envision actually come to pass. By acknowledging anxiety, and recognizing that it is unfounded in most cases, one can keep fears in perspective. When you feel anxiety creeping up and your courage slipping away, ask yourself, 'What is the worst thing that can happen, and what is the probability of this happening?' How many times has a waiter refused to allow you to return food that was cooked improperly? How many times have you actually been rejected because you told someone 'no'? Fortunately, 99 percent of our anxieties do not produce the consequences we anticipate.

By keeping your anxieties in perspective and practicing the techniques in this chapter you can learn to take risks, stand up for yourself, and avoid having people taking unfair advantage of you.

With time and practice, courage will become a natural way of conduct, both in business and in life. You will have the zest to actively take charge of your world!

# USING THE WBC
# CONCEPT

*'If you have faults, do not fear self-improvement.'*

Confucius

*Oz, left to himself, smiled to think of his success in giving the Scarecrow, the Tin Woodman, and the Lion exactly what they thought they wanted. 'How can I help being a humbug,' he said, 'when all these people made me do things that everybody knows can't be done? It was easy to make the Scarecrow, the Tin Woodman and the Lion happy because they imagined that I could do anything.'*

The Wizard of Oz
L. Frank Baum

People with a balanced WBC profile are confident, well-adjusted and self-reliant individuals. When things go wrong, rather than blame others for their failure, WBC people look to themselves for solutions. Research is always the foundation for action and WBC people amass information, collect data and work in a logical and determined manner. They organize their time well and set priorities. Sensitive to the needs and feelings of others, WBC people are cognizant of the fact that success seldom occurs in solitude. An ability to inspire and motivate others, combined with determination and persistence, characterizes the WBC person's pursuit of goals. Most importantly, they know how to take calculated chances and assume reasonable risks. Flexibility, not dogmatic rigidity, characterizes the WBC's astuteness, good-heartedness and determination when solving a problem. The ability to 'change gears', and to utilize a combination of wisdom, benevolence and courage, makes the WBC person truly unique. A well organized mind, a concern for people, and a strong desire to get things done separate them from the crowd.

## WBC DISEQUILIBRIUM
WBC Disequilibrium occurs when one dimension of the WBC profile submerges the other two. Dominant W people, deficient in benevolence and courage, may be knowledgeable and have good ideas. However, difficulties in dealing with people and a lack of assertiveness may inhibit success. People with a dominant B profile lack widom and courage and are disorganized and fearful of implementing ideas. These deficiencies discourage success. Dominant B people may reach positions of authority, but the organization rarely flourishes. Dominant C persons, deficient in wisdom and benevolence, would rather fight than figure out a plan that works with people. Although a C style may make a good warrior, in corporate life they create chaos.

The following three case studies illustrate how failure occurs when one's dimensions are out of balance.

### High W, Low BC
Ever since he graduated from law school ten years ago, Frank worked obsessively for a large petrochemical corporation. Always

punctual, Frank worked hard, but always lagged behind in getting anything accomplished. When given an assignment he endlessly researched the subject, fearing a mistake would be costly to the corporation. Frank's meticulousness, a form of procrastination, went unnoticed until deadlines required the completion of work. Although unpaid, Frank frequently worked overtime and spent many hours in the library researching projects. At home he read law journals and business periodicals, clipping and filing all articles related to his work.

Frank was highly intelligent and belonged to the Mensa Society where he debated abstract philosophical ideas. Frank was a loner. Each day, he brought his lunch and ate in solitude while working on assignments and reports. A bachelor who lived with his mother, Frank had few social or recreational outlets. He enjoyed reading and spent much time fantasizing. When Frank took the WBC-Q his level of W was high, but he was low on B & C. This profile perfectly reflected his character — an isolated intellectual with few friends and a passive orientation to life. Frank's failure to develop benevolence and courage in his character led to his failure to progress up the corporate ladder.

## High B, Low WC

Can one be too benevolent? We all like people who exude warmth and good will. People who are agreeable, friendly and likeable often become politicians or enter professions that maximize their contacts with people. Generosity and compassion are not enough to ensure success. In the following case history, benevolence was Sarah's forte, but failure to develop wisdom and courage hindered her potential.

Sarah was a secretary in a large state university. She always smiled and had a good word for everyone. She was goodhearted and reliable, frequently doing favors and running errands for friends at work. Sarah was not a college graduate, and people at the university urged her to complete college. Sarah always refused, saying, 'I am just not smart enough.' Sarah was a follower, and was fearful of initiating anything. Several times she was promoted to administrative assistant to some important professor on the faculty; but things never seemed to work out, and Sarah was transferred back to the secretarial pool. Over the course of years, Sarah had seen many younger women move up in the university to higher paying jobs. And all the while, Sarah smiled.

Sarah's responses on the WBC-Q indicated low scores on W and C. Sarah was stuck on the first rung of the wisdom ladder. She could learn from others but was inhibited when it came to studying and especially independently applying knowledge. Her lack of wisdom was not due to low intelligence, but indicated a lack of confidence in her ability to learn. Timidity and a lack of courage were responsible for Sarah's self-effacing behavior and her insistence that she could not learn. Sarah's success at the university was limited by her failure to develop W and C. Secretly, Sarah desired more respect and the prestige associated with advancement and resented the younger women who were promoted over her.

### High C, Low WB

Fearlessness reflects audacity and boldness, the qualities of a 'go-getter', and is usually reflected in the reaping of great rewards. However, untempered forthrightness and impulsiveness are counter-productive. In the following case history a failure to blend wisdom and benevolence with courage proved to be George's downfall.

George, a junior executive in a utility company, constantly bragged that he always told the truth. He was proud of this character trait and frequently proclaimed, 'If the truth hurts, that is just tough.' Outspoken during business meetings, George had the reputation of talking before thinking. He was honest, hardworking and believed that these attributes were the keys to success. When told by his immediate supervisor that he was too blunt with subordinates, George became indignant, protesting, 'If people can't take the truth without getting upset about criticism, then they are not tough enough or good enough to work for this company.'

George did not understand why he was passed over for promotion, and bitterly complained to peers that the company did not appreciate an honest expression of opinion. George's scores on the WBC-Q indicated a high C with low scores on W and B. George failed to appreciate that his style of management greatly impedes productivity because it engenders fear and anger. Unfortunately for

George his ignorance of wise and benevolent management styles was responsible for his failure to be promoted.

## Discussion

It is obvious that deficiencies in wisdom, benevolence or courage can hinder success and lead to personal unhappiness. Frank, a highly intelligent man, was lacking in benevolence and courage. Wisdom alone was insufficient for promotion and Frank was a miserable man both at work and in his personal life. Behind the mask of smiling Sarah was a disconsolate woman deficient in wisdom and courage. George, with his directness and bluntness might have fared better as a combat soldier. Fortunately, for Frank, Sarah and George, all received personal counseling that emphasized the development and blending of WBC into their work and personal lives.

In order to help clarify the effective and ineffective characteristics associated with each style, refer to the chart below.

As you go through life, you will encounter a variety of people with combinations of these dimensions. The ability to interact with the varying dimensions is important to your success. The following sections on team building, dimension flexing and problem solving can assist you in handling those in disequilibrium.

## CHARACTERISTICS ASSOCIATED WITH DIMENSIONS

| Effective Characteristics | Ineffective Characteristics |
| --- | --- |
| **Wisdom** | |
| Astute | Priggish |
| Conservative | Rigid |
| Analytical | Paralysis of analysis |
| Precise | Unjustifiably critical |
| Perceptive | Guileful |
| Judicious | Unfeeling |
| Deliberative | Indisposed to action |

**Benevolence**

| | |
|---|---|
| Empathetic | Puts people before task |
| Humane | Overly emotional |
| Generous | Blames self — feels guilty |
| Good listener | Concedes easily |
| Altruistic | Subjective |
| Feeling | Soft |
| Open with others | Indiscreet |

**Courage**

| | |
|---|---|
| Bold | Impulsive |
| Action-oriented | Puts task before people |
| Firm | Dogmatic |
| Assertive | Aggressive |
| Decisive | Under-plans |
| Unquestioning | Overpowers |
| Self-confident | Easily angered |

**Team Building**

A 'team' as it is used here, pertains to work groups such as a committee or task-force. Its membership consists of peers and their immediate supervisor. A 'team' must have a purpose, they must benefit from each other's experience or knowledge, and must agree to work together rather than in isolation. It is essential, in formulating a team, to consider the WBC profiles of each prospective member.

We tend to like people who are most like ourselves. People who have the same WBC profiles are most likely to get along with each other. For this reason, we like to choose people to work on our teams who have the same strengths and weaknesses as ourselves. This may make for a harmonious team with little interpersonal conflict, but it leaves the team with major weaknesses. For example, if a team is composed of people with predominately WB profiles, this team will analyze data and be friendly with each other, but they will not have the courage to implement solutions to problems. Similarly, if a team is predominately a CW profile, this team will be action-oriented and will analyze data, but they will give little consideration to the people being impacted by their actions.

Team members usually have the same dominant profile, although research shows a heterogeneous group will out-perform a homogeneous one. Using WBC profiles in team building can help establish a well-rounded team with increased effectiveness.

In order to identify the profile of a potential team member, one may either give them the WBC questionnaire contained in this book or, try to identify the person's profile by their personality characteristics. Listed below are some characteristics as they relate to each profile. Remember, always look for as many profile characteristics as possible when trying to identify a profile.

### Identifying Profiles: Wisdom

People with a dominant wisdom profile dress in conservative, formal clothing. The three-piece suit, white shirt and wing-tipped shoes are frequently seen. They have a limited use of gestures, few facial expressions and move rigidly. Wisdom profiles are serious, reserved and are able to control the expression of their feelings. As a manager, they will supervise in a disciplined manner, showing more interest in a task than people. Decisions are based on facts rather than emotions.

Their office decor is on the barren side, having few pictures on the wall and an absence of memorabilia. Desks are neatly organized and colors are subdued. Charts, graphs, reference books and technical credentials may be seen.

### Benevolence

People with a dominant benevolent profile adapt their choice of clothing to the situation. They mainly dress to please others. One may frequently see contemporary clothing that is colorful and somewhat casual. Their gestures, facial expressions and movements are animated and lively. As a manager they supervise in a personal manner, have less structure in their use of time and allow feelings to have a great influence on decision making.

Office decor tends toward a 'homey' atmosphere. Family portraits and snapshots are usually seen. Office colors lean toward the warmer colors. Their desk may have toys, gimmicks, or memorabilia on it. Benevolent people like to read novels, autobiographies and other human interest stories.

## Courage

People with a dominant courage profile dress for action, sleeves rolled up, top button of their shirt loose with their tie pulled down. Their eye contact is over-extended and in some extreme cases, a piercing glare. Voice tone is sharp; sentences, short stacattos. They are poor listeners, frequently interrupting the speaker and may even finish sentences for others.

As a manager they can be authoritarian, like a fast pace, and do more than one thing at a time.

Office decor is cluttered or even messy. Being action-oriented, the courageous person does not take time to put files, books or other materials back into their proper places after using them. Pictures indicate competitiveness or an action orientation. Courageous people have little time for reading, but when they do, they read capsulized material such as *Reader's Digest* or *Newsweek*.

Most people will be different combinations of these various characteristics. Dimensions flexing is a skill that will help you identify the ten different WBC profiles and use this knowledge to improve interpersonal relationships.

## Dimension Flexing

Dimension flexing is doing what is appropriate for the situation by temporarily using some dimensions of one's non-dominant profiles.

It is a means of communicating in a way that is more readily acceptable to persons of another profile. Body language, choice of words, length and degree of formality and emotional tone are considered when using dimension flexing. The goal does not change; the way in which you communicate does, although not radically. A few changes in the way you approach an important customer, boss, vendor, or associate will make your exchange more palatable to them. No one is just one or two dimensions to the total exclusion of the others.

When something important is at stake, communicate on the same wavelength as the person you wish to influence. Do this by first identifying the profile of the listener. If they have a profile different from yours, tap into and emphasize your non-dominant traits. This does not mean a radical departure of the way you normally act. Such extreme changes are apt to damage a relationship. Dimension flexing is simply accenting the behaviors you have in common with the other person.

Confucius said, 'The relation between superiors and inferiors is like that between wind and grass. The grass must bend when the wind blows over it.'

In dimension flexing it is suggested that you become like the grass when dealing with someone that you wish to influence. One needs to bend their own profile to a degree in order to succeed with the person with a profile different from their own.

For example, suppose that you are a strong W and your immediate supervisor is a strong C, what behaviors could you select from the C profile to add to your repertoire that would enhance your effectiveness in dealing with your supervisor? One suggestion is to always get to the point without using unnecessary verbiage or explanations. High W profiles make long, formal presentations during which they present several alternatives to a given problem and they carefully weigh the pros and cons of each of the alternatives. High C profiles, on the other hand, consider this approach non-assertive. They prefer presentations that are short and informal during which the one best solution is presented. By eliminating all of the unessential data that the C profile doesn't want to hear anyway, the employee can be far more successful in dealing with the supervisor.

Confucius said, 'The gentleman can influence those above him; the small man can only influence those below him.'

Anyone put into the position of manager, with the power to hire, fire, promote, increase salaries, etc., will find that influencing subordinates a rather easy task. The power of the position will usually do most of the influencing. When the manager attempts to influence superiors, the characteristics of the manager become all important.

Another example: suppose you had to sell a product to a customer whose profile was BW and your profile is a C. Some personality conflicts are likely to develop. If the BW customer is approached in the usual C manner, e.g. hard-driving, fast-talking, off-the-cuff, the BW is likely to be turned off. By practicing dimension flexing, the C could select a few characteristic behaviors from the BW profile and add them to his repertoire. The C in relating to the BW may consciously strive to be more personable and considerate. The C may take some time to plan and organize their presentation rather than using their usual off-the-cuff presentation style. A few changes in behavior such as making a few personal remarks and using charts or graphs to illustrate a point could help establish cooperation and rapport with the BW customer.

What follows is an exercise designed to test your ability to identify the different profiles and to test your use of dimension flexing.

## Identifying Profiles

Read the following descriptions and identify the profile of the main character. Also, decide what approach would be best if you were making a presentation to this person.

1. Henry reprimanded someone every 15 minutes. He was constantly feeling time pressure to meet deadlines and to get things accomplished. He was blunt with others regardless of the effect on their feelings. People who would not get to the point, or who fed him meaningless data irritated him. His production rate was higher than any other department, but so was his turnover rate.

    What is Henry's profile? What would be the best approach in making a presentation to him?

2. You go to see Tim Simmons, who is a potential new customer. Tim comes out to the outer office to greet you with a handshake. You mention that you share a mutual acquaintance

and he brightens perceptibly. You follow him into an office painted in warm colors and notice technical journals on his desk and a flip-chart displaying bar graphs in one corner. On his neatly organized desk is a calculator.

What is Tim's probable profile and what is your best approach?

3. You are having lunch with a friend. In response to the question, 'How are things going in the Purchasing Department?' he responds by telling you about the problems he is having with Steve, his boss.

'Steve usually wants things done immediately with reams of supporting data. I know little about his personal life and when I talk about personal matters Steve seems impatient and usually changes the subject to more technical shop-talk. All he is concerned with is, "When can we get it done and does this make sense?"

What is Steve's probable profile and how would you advise your friend in establishing better relations with his boss?

4. A receptionist shows you into a vendor's office. The man behind the desk remains seated. He is dressed in a three-piece conservative suit. His desk is bare, except for one pad of paper with neatly written notes. You comment on an action picture of a boxing match on the wall behind him. He says, 'I understand you are here to make a presentation. Can we get on with it? I hope you have all of the supporting information.'

What is his probable profile and what is the best approach in making your presentation?

5. When you called on Anne, a potential customer, she started the conversation by asking if you knew several people in the community. She then asked if you wanted a cup of coffee. Her first question concerning your business was, 'What kind of relations does your company have in the community?'

What is Anne's probable profile and how shall you approach your presentation?

6. For the first time in your career, you are going to meet Mr. Barth, the President of your company. You are to present a new

customer incentive plan that you have worked on for two years. Mr. Barth has a reputation for being a nice guy that gets things done. He stands up and shakes your hand when you meet him. He then says, 'Let's hear this new plan you've been working on.'

What is Mr. Barth's probable profile and how should you approach your presentation?

7. You are making a presentation to a major customer with a multi-million dollar account. Because of the importance of this account, you arrive early, but the receptionist shows you in at the exact appointment time. The customer looks at his watch and says, 'I kept you waiting because I have a precisely planned schedule.' You notice that he is dressed in a dark conservative suit and his office has a plain look about it. He says, 'Shall we begin with the detailed audit of your services.'

What is the customer's probable profile and how should you proceed with your presentation?

8. You are going to see the urban planning commissioner to ask for a re-zoning of some property you recently purchased. When you go into her office, you notice a ream of computer data neatly stacked on her credenza and a personal computer on her desk. Everything is neatly organized and she is dressed with conservative good taste. The commissioner shakes your hand and inquires about your family.

What is the commissioner's probable profile and how should she be approached?

9. You volunteered to work for the United Way for a local fund drive. If you get the support of the president of the largest corporation in the state, it will mean a major contribution. You arrive at his office and he greets you at the door, giving you an energetic handshake and whisks you into his office. After a few personal exchanges he asks what he can do for you.

What is his probable profile and how should you approach your presentation?

10. You have been unemployed for six months. The finance company is threatening foreclosure on your house and your

wife is eight months pregnant. As you sit in your living room worrying and watching a soap opera, the phone rings. The caller says that a position similar to your previously· held position has just developed. If interested, you can be scheduled for a panel interview at 9 a.m. the following day. The panel interview is to consists of six interviewers taking turns asking questions. How should you present yourself?

## Answers to the Identifying Profiles Exercise:

1. Henry is a C profile. He is quick to reprimand subordinates and has a chronic sense of time urgency coupled with a sense of anger toward anyone or anything that prevents his immediate gratification. The feelings of others are rarely considered as he bluntly tells subordinates what he wants them to do. People who do not get to the point quickly irritate Henry. His subordinates work hard out of fear of Henry's wrath, but they seldom develop loyalty. For this reason his production rate is high but so is his turnover rate.

   With a C you must be direct, to the point and concise. Never approach a C with a list of alternatives. Pick the one best solution and forcefully support your choice. Tap their competitive spirit in order to get their enthusiastic support. Do not bother them with a lot of data or details. All they really want to know is bottom-line information, i.e., when can you get it to me, how much will it cost and what is the return on investment.

2. Tim is a BW profile. Tim's warm reception when you arrived at his office is a clear indication of benevolence. Sharing a common acquaintance is a definite plus when establishing rapport with a B. Many times B's dress in warm colors and have similar colors in their office decor. The technical journals, flip charts displaying bar graphs and a neatly organized desk with a calculator are all accouterments of Tim's W dimension. W's are naturally fastidious and have an inclination toward graphs, calculators and other analytical tools.

   With a BW you must be personal and be prepared. Make personal contact before starting your formal presentation. Try to achieve mutually agreed upon goals. Show how your ideas or product will affect people. Offer personal assurance that doing things the way you have proposed is the best possible decision. List the pros and cons of each alternative solution.

3. Steve is a CW profile. A sense of time urgency paradoxically coupled with a need for insistent data gathering is the hallmark of a CW profile. They usually avoid talking about personal issues and close, intimate, relationships are formed slowly. Their main need is to accomplish tasks in an orderly, logical way.

   In dealing with CWs do not waste time on personal exchanges. Get to the point immediately, and be prepared for many direct questions. Be as formal as possible without being overly wordy. Emphasize action, demonstrate bottom-line impact, be logical and have supporting information.

4. The vendor is a WC profile. A lack of benevolence is indicated when the vendor remained seated behind his desk when you entered his office. A more benevolent person would have stood up, shook your hand and/or made a personal remark or inquiry. The conservative suit, the barren desk, and the neatly written notes are indications of the W profile. The action picture of the boxing match and the vendor's urgent insistence that you get on with your presentation are C profile characteristics.

   With a WC you have to make an organized presentation with some details. After going through the pros and cons of each alternative solution, make a strong stand for the one best alternative. Don't waste time on personal chit-chat, be on time and quickly get into your presentation.

5. Anne is a B profile. Establishing a common acquaintance is a social ritual for the B profile when first meeting someone. They want to know where you have previously lived, worked or went to school so that shared remembrances can be discussed. In this way the B profile develops a sense of trust and rapport. Anne's first question concerning, 'what kind of relations does your company have with the community', indicate a greater concern for what others think rather than the task to accomplish.

In approaching a B be sure to establish person to person contact before making your presentation. Shake hands, make good eye contact and invite personal conversation. Encourage the expression of any doubts or fears they may have. Always relate how your proposal or product affects people. Do not use pressure, manipulation or the hard-sell.

6. Mr Barth is a BC profile. His reputation of being a nice guy indicates a B profile characteristic, and getting things done indicates a C profile characteristic. Standing up and shaking your hand is the warm greeting one would expect from a B profile. After the initial greeting the need to get down to business and hear your new plan indicates a C profile.

   When meeting a BC give them a firm handshake and make good eye contact. BC's respond to enthusiasm and like high energy presentations. Be entertaining and spike your presentation with humor. Use personal experiences and testimonials from others to illustrate your points. End your presentation with assurances that everyone is going to love the outcome, and give them an action plan for implementation.

7. The customer's profile is W. Precision concerning plans, schedules and data is a universally shared characteristic among Ws. They dress in conservative good taste and their office is usually neat and somewhat barren or plain. They demand all the details when engaged in a decision-making process.

   With a W, weigh the pros and cons of each alternative solution to any given problem. Make your presentations formal, using flip charts with graphs and pie-charts. Don't talk about personal issues. Be prepared, systematic and logical. Be on time, not early and not late.

8. The commissioner's profile is WB. The reams of computer data and the personal computer are some of the analytical tools that the WB are predisposed toward. The neat organization of her office and conservative dress further indicate a W profile. The handshake and personal inquiry about your family are B profile characteristics.

   You should be prepared with an organized presentation. Do not try to circumvent personal exchanges such as inquiries about the family, or other personal matters. These pleasantries are important to the WB profile. While presenting the pros and cons of each alternative, always include how each alternative will affect people involved with the problem.

9. The President is a CB profile. The energy in the handshake and the time urgency of getting you into his office indicate a C profile. The warmth of his greeting and the few personal exchanges are B characteristics. The cutting off of the personal exchanges to get down to business is a reversion back to his dominant profile.

   Your best approach is to charge into your presentation with great enthusiasm and vigor and make a strong appeal for emotional support. Emphasize action and let the CB know how their actions will affect people. Have a firm handshake and good eye contact. Do not list alternatives, but choose one solution and support it with assertiveness.

10. Because the panel has six members, the chances of several different profiles being present is likely. You should therefore demonstrate the well-rounded WBC profile. Be on time and prepared. Make a few personal exchanges before beginning the interview. Have supporting material available to present in case of detailed questions. The presentation of yourself should flow logically to a conclusion. Do not forget to mention how well you work with people. Finally, emphasize your potential impact on company profitability as their employee.

## THE WBC WAY TO DRESS
Confucius said, 'A gentleman does not wear facings of purple or mauve, nor in undress does he use pink or roan. In hot weather he wears an unlined gown of fine thread loosely woven, but puts on an outside garment before going out-of-doors. With a black robe, he wears black lambskin. With a yellow robe, fox fur. On his undress robe the fur cuffs are long; but the right is shorter than the left. His bed clothes must be half as long again as a man's height. The thicker kinds of fox and badger are for home wear. Except when in mourning, he wears all his girdle-ornaments. Apart from his court apron, all his skirts are wider at the bottom than at the waist.

Lambskin dyed black and a hat of dark-dyed silk must not be worn when making visits of condolence. At the announcement of the new moon, he must go to Court in full Court dress.'

Confucius had a prescribed way of appropriate attire in his society as we have a prescribed way in ours. The width of our lapels, the color of the shirt, the pattern of tie we choose, and hundreds of other aspects of our apparel combine to form a powerful impression on others. Our dimension profiles determine to a great extent how we choose to dress. Successful dressing is no more than acquiring the right clothing so as to reflect a balanced WBC profile. Our profiles determine virtually every choice we make in life: what profession we choose, what TV shows we watch, what books we read, what hobbies we pursue and what clothes we choose to wear.

When dressing for that all important interview, or when dressing for everyday business affairs, consider the following suggestions:

W profiles dress with cold conservatism. Their wardrobe lacks color and is stiff and formal. They would benefit by adding a dash of color to their apparel such as a red or maize tie or scarf with matching handkerchief in the jacket pocket. Occasionally wearing a sports coat or shirt-waist dress instead of the usual suit will instill a bit of the B profile. Do not be hesitant to take off your coat and roll up your shirt sleeves when there are intense deadline pressures. This symbolizes that you are getting down to business and adds a touch of the C profile to your appearance.

WB profiles dress in a conservative style with warm colors but they do not have an action orientation. To add the missing touch of C, try not buttoning your suit or jacket when walking, unbutton the top button of your shirt and loosen your tie or scarf, and occasionally roll up your shirt sleeves. Men should add a bold striped shirt to their wardrobe and a sporty watch. Women should wear prints and stripes rather than large, floral designs.

WC profiles also dress conservatively but usually appear disheveled. Not much thought is given to color, therefore, colors may range from warm to cold. This profile would benefit from more consideration as to how their appearance affects others. Make an effort to color coordinate your clothing. Men should wear an occasional sport coat and update their lapels and ties. Women can add a belt or scarf to enhance color and affect.

B profiles dress in contemporary clothing with the hope that other people will not find them offensive. They have a propensity toward warmer colors and slip-on shoes. Sport coats and dresses rather than suits are preferred. It would be beneficial to dress in suits occasionally and to wear more conservative colors. Men should consider lace-up shoes and women low-heeled pumps.

BW profiles dress in contemporary clothing with definite conservative styling. They lack an action orientation in their dress. To add a touch of C they should roll up their shirt sleeves and loosen their ties when there are deadline pressures. Men could add a bold striped shirt and a sporty watch to their wardrobe. Women should choose dark, rich colors rather than pastels. The BW profile is very similar to the WB profile. They differ in that the WB profile is more stiff and formal than the BW profile.

BC profiles dress in warm contemporary clothing with a definite informal bearing. Wearing occasional suits, with buttoned jackets and starched shirts would benefit the BC man. Colors should be toned down and accessories should be simple. Care should be taken in choosing more conservative styles and darker, less flamboyant colors. Women should wear jewelry sparingly and avoid trendy styles.

C profiles, no matter where they work, dress as if they were working in a production room. How they dress is of little concern to them. Disheveled, messy and uncoordinated characterize their style of dress. C profiles would benefit by having their clothes cleaned and pressed more frequently, buttoning their jackets when walking, and keeping their ties pulled tight. Men should wear suits more than sport coats and white or blue shirts rather than brash colors. Warmer colors should be chosen for suits and sport coats. Women should wear suits that are carefully color coordinated and adopt a hairstyle that is neat in appearance and easily maintained.

CW profiles are usually disheveled, but wear conservative, traditional styles. The CW is more messy in dress than the WC. This profile would benefit by choosing warmer colors and more contemporary accessories. Their tendency to wear the same clothing for years results in an outdated appearance. Updating their wardrobe every two years would be beneficial.

CB profiles tend to dress informally in contemporary styles. They temper the tendency toward dishevelment with their concern to please others. The CB profile would benefit from choosing more traditional styles in clothing and by toning down the colors they wear. Men should button their coats when walking and keep their ties pulled up taut. Women would benefit from a more tailored look and classic, understated jewelry and accessories.

This outline of attire can be an aid in identifying the dimension of others. This should not be the only clue you use in identifying profiles. Company dress codes, how the boss dresses, and how a spouse wants his/her mate to dress can influence choices in clothing. Always look for as many clues as possible when identifying a profile.

The Wizard of Oz knew the importance of his appearance when he created the impression of being all powerful. You, too, can dress in a way that will enhance your chances to succeed in business and in life by following these simple guidelines.

## WBC OBJECTIVES

This is a typical W profile activity, but if done with WBC principles in mind can become a tremendously useful tool in business and in life. In the chapter on developing wisdom, you did an exercise in Goal Setting. Now, do the same exercise for your department or organization. Imagine yourself at your own retirement party. You have received your gold watch, a round of applause, and now it is time for a speech. What major accomplishments would you cite to your fellow workers? On a blank sheet of paper list four major accomplishments you would like to achieve prior to retirement.

In the next exercise, imagine it is one year from now and you are sitting in your boss's office receiving a performance appraisal. On a sheet of paper list four projects you would like to accomplish during the coming year. Now imagine it is one month from now and you are writing your monthly activities report. List four accomplishments you would like to have completed within the coming month.

Look back over your list of both long and short term objectives and ask yourself the following questions:

— Do my objectives represent a sufficient task for the period?

— Are my objectives obtainable within the measuring period?

— Do my short-run and long-run objectives support each other?

— Have I considered both the qualitative as well as the quantitative aspects of my objectives?

If you answered 'No' to any one of these questions, rethink and reformulate your objectives.

With the W aspects of your planning and analyzing objectives accomplished, turn your attention to the B aspects of your objectives. Re-examine your objectives and ask yourself the following questions for each objective:

— Are my objectives in harmony with my organization's objectives?

— Are my objectives stated clearly and simply so they can be easily communicated to my boss and my subordinates?

— Have I considered how much time away from friends and family will be needed to accomplish these objectives?

— Do I have the support of my staff to accomplish these objectives?

Again rethink and reformulate your objectives if you answered 'No' to any of these questions.

Finally, consider the C aspects of your objectives. Re-examine each objective and ask yourself the following questions:

— Are my objectives measurable, lending themselves to evaluation?

— Do I have in mind a step-by-step action plan for accomplishing my objectives?

— Do I feel confident in my abilities and the abilities of my staff to attain my objectives?

— Do I feel strongly enough about my objectives to tenaciously pursue them?

Rethink and reformulate your objectives if you answered 'No' to any of these questions.

You now have a WBC set of objectives. The advantage of doing this exercise is that you now know specifically what you need to do. Since your goals are firmly set, your performance toward goal attainment will be enhanced. Your goals as an individual will be more realistic and tied closer to the organizations' goals.

One word of caution: writing objectives may make the commitment toward that specifically worded goal more firm. This may result in the desire to tenaciously adhere to the goal. As the world and your organization change, so should your goals. As Confucius says, 'The only ones who do not change are sages and idiots.' Repeat this exercise whenever you feel that your goals are out of sync with your environment. By doing this your goals will remain responsive to the world around you.

After setting your objectives you may encounter some problems in achieving them. Confucius said, 'If a man does not give thought to problems which are still distant he will be worried by them when they come nearer.'

In the next section, you will learn to solve problems the WBC way.

## WBC PROBLEM SOLVING AND DECISION MAKING SYSTEM

Most managers spend more time making personnel decisions than any other kind of decision. This is well justified, because no other decisions are so long-lasting in their consequences or so difficult to change. The estimated success rate for personnel decisions is about 30 percent. Only one-third of the personnel decisions managers make actually work. One-third are minimally effective, and the remaining third are outright failures. The failure rate is a direct reflection on the bias caused by our dominant dimension, which has been formed by past experience. The W profile analyzes the job description and the applicant's resume, but fails to interview the applicant with empathy and understanding. The B profile listens with empathy and understanding during the interview but fails to understand the technical needs and objectives of the position. The C profile makes decisive personnel decisions without fully analyzing the risk of a poor decision. In order to overcome these natural profile limitations we need a system that is designed so that one is compelled to consider the viewpoints of other dimensions.

Confucius said, 'A gentleman can see a question from all sides without bias. The small man is biased and can see a question only from one side.'

We perceive questions through the filters of our profiles. It is through this perception that our biases are formed. Our profile is the prime determinant of our behavior. It determines our choice of clothes in the morning, our chosen profession, and how we approach a question or problem. Unless we have an extremely well-rounded profile, chances are we will not see a question from all sides. Therefore, we need a system that encourages us to see what other profiles see naturally.

This problem-solving system is designed for a team of three to seven people and may be adapted to any problem regardless of its size or difficulty. For complicated or multi-faceted problems, the system may be used in successive rounds on different aspects of the problem through step five, then the various choices can be intergrated into a coordinated plan of implementation. Do not skip any steps in using this model. Each step is designed to counteract a unidimensional weakness.

### Step 1: Profile Awareness
When confronted with problems as an individual or as a group, our WBC profiles should be taken into account. When groups are formed the likely consistency is for the group to be composed of similar dimensions. Ws like other Ws, Bs like other Bs and Cs like other Cs. For this reason, most groups are homogeneous rather than heterogeneous (see team building on page 93). When solving problems, better results will be achieved if a group has representatives from every dimension. A unidimensional individual faces the same difficulties as a homogeneous group. There are three basic reasons why homogeneous groups and unidimensional individuals frequently make poor decisions.
1. The group or individual who lacks courage will assume that the problem is bigger than their ability. Even if they arrive at a decision, the implementation plan will be lacking.
2. Groups or individuals who lack wisdom never develop their problem solving skills. They ignore the problem until it is too late to do anything about it.
3. Groups or individuals who lack benevolence reject tentative solutions before giving them a thorough hearing; consequently reducing their own desire or the desire of other group members to contribute more solutions. They blame others for the problem in the first place.

## Step II: Acknowledge there is a Problem and Decide to Find a Solution

Before any action can be taken to resolve the problem, we must acknowledge its existence. But this is not enough — we must also decide to do something about it. Many of us know we are overweight, drink too much alcohol, smoke cigarettes or have an unproductive employee, but we continue to allow things to go unchanged. What is lacking is the courage to make the decision to do something about the problem. Once we clearly decide there is a problem and that we are going to do something about it, writing the problem down and telling others will help us muster up the courage to change the status quo.

## Step III: Define the Problem

A 'problem' is any condition in which a person or group experiences a sense of unease; things are not as they should be, or as we wish them to be. When we 'define' the problem we provide clarity instead of clouded thinking, understanding instead of confused feelings and commonality of purpose. How a problem is defined will either expand or limit the possible solution. For example, if you say, 'My car has broken down, so I must buy a new one', you have set some definite problem parameters. Within the problem definition, you have decided that you will buy a 'car' and not a truck, that it will be a 'new' car and not a used one, and that you are not going to fix your old car. If the problem is restated to say, 'My car has broken down and I must have transportation to get to work,' you have expanded the problem definition to include many alternatives: fixing the old car, car pooling, public transportation, or buying some other type of vehicle. It is desirable to define problems in a way that will not limit the alternatives for solution.

Before starting to solve a problem, be sure the problem is stated accurately and precisely. Pinpoint the defective object or problem situation and state exactly what is wrong. This process not only keeps us on track, but it also helps focus the search for relevant data.

Those with a high C profile have the most trouble with this step. They jump to conclusions, making snap decisions as to the cause of a problem rather than spending adequate time and effort defining it.

## Step IV: Decide on a Method to Work on the Problem

Some alternatives are: form a committee, call in a consultant, hold a conference with all those affected by the problem, form a task force, or solve it without anyone else's input. For many organizational problems, the third method, that of holding a conference with all affected by the problem, is the best method. Those with a vested interest will work harder for a solution and will support the solution with greater zeal if they feel ownership for the final action. The scope, importance and urgency of the problem should be considered when deciding on which method to apply. Remember, when using a group method it is best to include representatives from each WBC profile. Long drawn out meetings are counterproductive and often lead to sluggish thinking. A time limit of not more than two hours should be set. Those with a high B profile will revel in the group problem solving process. Some control should be exercised with high C profiles because they will try to dominate the group. High W profiles have the hardest time staying within time limitations. They may be overly verbose and insist on collecting more and more information before making a decision.

## Step V: Brainstorming

Brainstorming is one way of looking at a question from all sides. In brainstorming you are encouraged to forget bias, so your mind will be free to consider a new way to answer a question. The principles and rules to follow in brainstorming are as follows:

1. Try to produce a large number of ideas. Ideas generate other ideas. Postpone critical judgement of ideas until later. High C profiles should practice dimension flexing and suppress their urge to be overly critical.
2. Far-fetched ideas have value in that while an idea may be unsuitable in itself, it may serve as a thought-provoker for other, more suitable ideas. High W profiles will enjoy this if they have enough courage to express their ideas.
3. Everyone in the group is afforded an equal opportunity to participate. People with a low C profile tend to be shy and too reserved to freely express their ideas. Moving in a clockwise manner around the table, individuals are encouraged to contribute their ideas. Those who don't wish to comment simply

say, 'pass'. By verbally saying, 'pass', there is added assurance that no one is missed. On the following round, a member that had previously passed may now have an idea to express.

4. Someone in the group should be designated as the scribe. The scribe should be careful to record everything and be non-judgmental of the ideas of others. High B's make excellent scribes. They are good listeners and can remain non-critical.

## Step VI: Selecting a Solution

Selecting a solution by consensus is a group method in which all parties involved actively discuss the issues surrounding the decision. The group, with its conglomeration of diverse profiles, agrees to support the final decision. The ideas and feelings of all members are integrated into that decision thereby producing a feeling of ownership for the solution.

Decision by consensus is sometimes difficult to attain and will consume more time than other methods of selecting a solution. As the energies of the group become focused on the problem, the quality of the decision is enhanced. This approach results in a significantly higher-quality decision than other methods such as the use of majority power (voting), minority power (persuasion) and compromise.

In the consensus process, each group member is asked to:

1. Prepare their position prior to the group meeting with the realization that missing data will be supplied by other members. (The high W profiles are at their best in this phase of the process.)

2. Recognize an obligation to express an opinion and explain it fully. (The high C profile has no problem letting people know their opinions.)

3. Listen to the opinions and feelings of others and be open enough to modify your own position on the basis of logic and understanding. (The high B profile has the natural ability to listen with empathy).

4. Avoid conflict-reducing techniques such as voting, compromising, or giving in to keep the peace. Realize that differences of opinion are essential in data gathering. After everyone has contributed to the data pool, the best solution will become apparent.

**Step VII: The Action Plan**

This plan contains what specifically will be done. Assignments should be made to the individual responsible for implementation and an exact date assigned for the accomplishment of each phase of the action plan. In making assignments, choose people who have a stake in the successful resolution of the problem. (Those with a high C profile have no problem making assignments).

**Step VIII: Evaluate the Results**

One person in the group should be designated as 'evaluator'. Their function is to follow-up and make sure everyone is accomplishing their objectives. If the problem still exists or some new problems have been uncovered, the group may need to take further action. That action could be a continued commitment to work on the problem or a return to Step II, Redefining the problem.

Even when the problem has been solved, follow-up is helpful to the group and to the organization. A special effort by those with a low B profile should be made to give a word of appreciation to those who helped make the solution work.

**FOR INDIVIDUAL USE**

The WBC Problem Solving and Decision Making System can be used by individuals as well as groups.

In Step 1 — Profile Awareness, the individual must not only be aware of his profile, but must also do something about any profile limitations. If the individual is low in W, a special effort should be made to plan, understand the technical aspects of the problem, and to fully analyze the risk of each alternative. If low in B, the individual should consider the effect of each of their alternatives on people. If low in C, an emphasis on implementation is encouraged. Unless an alternative is chosen and a plan implemented, nothing gets accomplished.

A group of people is not needed in Step II — Acknowledgement of the problem; or in Step III — Define the problem.

Step IV — Decide on a method to work on the problem can be eliminated because you have already decided to work on the problem without anyone else's input.

Step V — Brainstorming can be accomplished by an individual

if one is not overly critical of his own ideas. The individual simply sits in a quiet room with a pad and pen. After a few deep relaxation breaths, the mind is allowed to run free. As ideas and alternatives come to mind, write them down paying little attention to spelling, grammar, or sentence structure. Do not reject any ideas even if they appear silly or inappropriate.

Step VI — Selecting a solution as an individual is somewhat different from selecting a solution in a group. Each alternative needs to be considered against each WBC dimension. For each alternative ask yourself, 'Have I collected enough information and have I done an adequate analysis of the consequences of choosing this alternative', 'Have I considered how this alternative will affect people', 'Do I have the resources for implementation of this alternative?' An organized way of screening each alternative is to create a matrix with these questions on the left side of the page and each alternative across the top. This will serve as an aid to counter any dimensional weaknesses in your WBC profile.

An individual with a low C should make an extra effort in Step VII — The Action Plan. Put your plan in writing and set deadlines for the accomplishment of each phase. Telling other people what you plan to do will serve as a reinforcer for plan accomplishment.

In Step VIII — Evaluating the results; the individual assumes the role of Evaluator. By periodically re-reading the action plan and comparing what you said you would do with what has actually been accomplished, an objective assessment can be made.

## THE WBC PROBLEM SOLVER

The WBC problem solver has the basic skills and positive attitudes to successfully solve problems. WBC people have the wisdom to carefully define the problem and generate viable alternatives; the benevolence to have respect for others and the ideas they generate; and the courage to accept the responsibility for their own actions. Problem solving skills will increase as one gains experience, particularly in successful problem solving. By using this system one can 'see a question from all sides without bias.' In *The Wizard of Oz*, Dorothy represents a good example of using the WBC profile to successfully solve her problem. By incorporating the Scarecrow's newfound wisdom, the Lion's courage and the Tin Woodman's benevolence, Dorothy was successful in returning to Kansas.

Recommendations in this chapter are aimed at improving your interpersonal skills and increasing your effectiveness on the job. The WBC concept has only three variables, so it can be used daily and spontaneously without the aid of this book as a reference. You may want to refer back for specific information when making a sale, forming a team or committee, setting objectives or solving a problem.

The basic WBC concept is concise enough so that you can keep it in mind and apply it throughout your life.

# POSTSCRIPT

If you have read and completed the exercises in this book, then you have incorporated into your life 2500 years of thought on human development. You have started with Confucius and traveled down the yellow brick road to gain heightened awareness of your own character in the use of wisdom, benevolence and courage.

You now have the ability to extend yourself, stretch your talents and become more valuable to yourself and your organization. You have a distinct advantage over those who have not yet learned how to manage their lives effectively. Your wisdom has increased by repeatedly climbing the wisdom ladder and by using the step-by-step study guide.

Responding to people with more understanding and sensitivity should be second nature. Forming lasting relationships, creating positive first impressions and having the power to motivate others are possible because of your asserted efforts to become more benevolent.

Increased confidence and backbone are yours, if you've made the effort to become more courageous. You can use the word 'no' without feeling guilty, anxious or uncomfortable. All of your communications with others can be improved if you have learned to stand up for yourself while not violating the rights of others.

By using the concept of dimension flexing, you have become aware of how perception affects communication, understanding, and productivity. Problem-solving and decision-making has become easier, more effective and accurate. By continuously incorporating the WBC Principles into your life, you will create a significant impact with everything you say and do.

Tzu-Kung asked Confucius, 'Is there any single saying that one can act upon all day and every day?'

Confucius said, 'Perhaps the saying about consideration: Never do to others what you would not like them to do to you.'